DEVOURED

Also by Amanda Marrone

Uninvited

Revealers

DEVOURED

Amanda Marrone

SIMON PULSE

New York   London   Toronto   Sydney

This book is a work of fiction. Any references to historical events, real people, or real locales are used fictitiously. Other names, characters, places, and incidents are the product of the author's imagination, and any resemblance to actual events or locales or persons, living or dead, is entirely coincidental.

SIMON PULSE

An imprint of Simon & Schuster Children's Publishing Division

1230 Avenue of the Americas, New York, NY 10020

First Simon Pulse paperback edition September 2009

Copyright © 2009 by Amanda Marrone

SIMON PULSE and colophon are registered trademarks of Simon & Schuster, Inc.

For information about special discounts for bulk purchases,

please contact Simon & Schuster Special Sales at 1-866-506-1949 or

business@simonandschuster.com.

The Simon & Schuster Speakers Bureau can bring authors to your live event. For more information or to book an event contact the Simon & Schuster Speakers Bureau at 1-866-248-3049 or visit our website at www.simonspeakers.com.

Designed by Mike Rosamilia

The text of this book was set in Adobe Caslon.

Manufactured in the United States of America

2 4 6 8 10 9 7 5 3 1

Library of Congress Cataloging-in-Publication Data

Marrone, Amanda.

Devoured / by Amanda Marrone. — 1st Simon Pulse pbk. ed.

p. cm.

Summary: Rising high school senior Megan has been haunted by her twin for ten years, but now Remy is trying to warn her about terrible danger surrounding Megan's summer job at an amusement park called the Land of Enchantment.

ISBN: 978-1-4169-7890-9 (pbk)

[1. Amusement parks—Fiction. 2. Ghosts—Fiction. 3. Death—Fiction. 4. Family problems—Fiction. 5. Characters in literature—Fiction. 6. Supernatural—Fiction.] I. Title.

PZ7.M3492Dev 2009

[Fic]—dc22

2009000287

ISBN: 978-1-4169-8540-2 (eBook)

This is for my father, Jerry Malloy, despite the fact
that he made me knock on mausoleum doors.
And no, getting ice cream afterward didn't make it better.
I still love you, though, Dad.

ACKNOWLEDGMENTS

Thanks to my so-scary-she's-perfect agent, Wendy Schmalz, and my spooktacular editor, Jen Klonsky, and all the folks at Simon Pulse. Thanks to my critique group: Pam Foarde, Rob Walsh, and especially Naomi Panzer, and Nina Nelson for rapid reading toward the end. And thanks to Kelsey Johnson Defatte for her never-ending support! I couldn't do it without you all!

Five Hundred Years Ago

"Helena," the large mirror beckoned from the east wall, "I have something of the utmost importance to show you."

Helena adjusted the crown on her head and scoffed. "I really don't think I need to see another damn dwarf pining away at the glass coffin."

"It's not that." The mirror flashed red with impatience. "Come and look."

Helena ignored the mirror's request and continued to gaze out at the meadows that had turned from dry brown to lush green seemingly overnight. "Mirror, did you know the girl used to love to run through the new spring grass?" She rolled her eyes. "With the birds twittering maddeningly after her." Helena thought it was through this same window that she'd felt the first pangs of envy—of hate.

No, not through the window, she decided, through the mirror. She pulled the fox stole tighter across her chest to guard against the cool breeze.

"My *queen*," the mirror implored, hoping a more formal tone would appease her. "You should see it for yourself, because . . ." It paused. The mirror had wanted to lure Helena to its glass and surprise her. It took great pleasure in seeing Helena's face contort with shock, but over the past few months, as Snow White had retained her beauty in the coffin, Helena had sunk into such a deep depression, the mirror could rarely entice her to look into it. But the mirror knew Snow White had been rescued—by a prince, no less—and surprised or not, Helena would be devastated by the news.

"She lives," the mirror whispered.

Helena inhaled and squeezed her eyes tightly shut. She knew this day would come. The girl simply would not die.

"So she lives," Helena said as a sharp pounding started in her temple. "You sound surprised." She rose from the window seat and approached the mirror. She looked at her reflection and plucked out a single white hair from among the black.

The mirror shimmered, casting Helena's image in a yellow light.

"Well, get on with it," she said. "Show me the girl, unless you're not done tormenting me with my fading looks."

"She lives and she will soon wed," the mirror stated matter-of-factly. "Preparations are already at hand, and a courier is on his way with an invitation."

A castle bustling with wedding activity appeared in the glass. Helena watched servants bring in armloads of ivy and heather for the floral arrangements. Snow White skipped into view, took a branch of heather from one of the maids, and waved it about as she danced past them into an open courtyard.

Helena shook her head and turned from the mirror. She rested her hand on the cool marble windowsill. "I'll be happy to attend Snow White's wedding," she said. "And I know the perfect gift." She walked back to the wall and ran her fingers along the mirror's gilded frame. "*You* will belong to Snow White."

"My queen, I belong to you!" the mirror protested.

Helena caught a quick glimpse of the creature that dwelled inside the mirror before her own reflection reappeared. She shuddered knowing that the long, hooked nose flanked by smoke-filled eyes would likely visit her in a nightmare tonight.

"Well," Helena said to the mirror, "I know how much you enjoy your hold on me, but you needn't worry. I have no doubt Snow White will succumb to your *charms* as easily as I did." She smiled. "Frankly, at this point, the prospect of you corrupting her soul is far more appealing than seeing her dead."

The mirror said nothing. It was already wondering just what would bring Snow White under its sway. Perhaps the knowledge that her prince had been intimate with many of the castle maids—some of whom were at this very moment sewing her wedding nightclothes—might prompt Snow White to seek out the mirror's special abilities for reassurance. Or spying.

The surface of the glass glimmered happily. Helena knew it was already counting the seconds until it could be alone with Snow White. She sighed. "If only the huntsman had done his job properly and carved out her heart when he was told to, I think I might have had a chance at happiness."

Helena's stomach turned. The mirror had told her she'd take in what she coveted the most—Snow White's beauty—by eating the girl's heart. She ran her fingers over the coarse hair poking out of her chin, hating to think of what she'd gained by eating the boar's heart the hunter had presented her with instead.

She looked out at the forest surrounding the fields. The huntsman fled when she asked how it was possible Snow White was cavorting with dwarves if he had indeed removed her heart. She caught sight of a small wisp of smoke floating up over some trees in the distance and wondered if that was where he was hiding. "I wish I could give *him* a gift as well," she said.

The mirror flashed in anticipation. Unlike some of its

previous owners, Helena had never guessed its true nature. She'd never divined that it could have done away with Snow White long ago if only she had wished it aloud.

Helena curled her hands into tight balls. "I wish he could feel the envy that haunts me night and day, the all-consuming longing for what others have." Helena laughed crazily. "I wish his kin *and* Snow White could feel this burning in their souls *forever.*"

Helena shook her head and sighed again. "In the meantime, I guess I'll have the seamstress cut me a new dress and have some shoes made." She looked at the mirror and smiled bitterly. "I hope you bring as much joy to Snow White's life as you have to mine."

She left the room, and the jinn that resided in the mirror granted the wish Helena unwittingly cast. It sent out a spell that reached around outcrops of rocks and twisted through brambles until it found the huntsman turning a skinned rabbit on a spit. The spell swirled around the man, and he paused as the hair on his arms stood on end. He scanned the thicket, thinking a wolf was lurking, perhaps drawn by the smell of roasting meat.

Having found its first mark, the spell wound its way around the trees to the next kingdom where it found the girl with skin as white as snow singing happily in the palace gardens. It wrapped around her heart, and she gasped, not knowing why she felt so uneasy just days before she was to wed her beloved prince.

Back at the castle, the mirror gleamed with pleasure. It then thought of Helena and wondered if it should warn her about what it had seen in the future—iron shoes, red-hot from lying in a bed of coals, placed on her feet at Snow White's wedding reception. It saw Helena dancing in the enchanted shoes until she took her last breath. The mirror pondered its ability to change her destiny, but in the end it decided that if Helena really wanted to see her stepdaughter wed, who was it to stop her?

～ ONE ～

Nicki rounds the corner fast, and I clutch the armrest tightly. I take a deep breath and see her look my way.

"Oh God, sorry," she says as she takes her foot off the gas pedal and presses on the brake. "I get carried away on this stretch."

I look out at the river hugging the road and will myself to take in the gorgeous White Mountains scenery instead of imagining the car skidding off into the water. "Hey, no problem," I lie. "And thanks for driving me. Figures my mom has one of her stupid dog things the day I get the interview. She and Fergus have a new routine, and this is the first time they're performing it."

Nicki laughs. "How could she retire the 'Toxic' number? That was a showstopper!"

"Ha, ha, funny."

Of course my mom dancing with our golden retriever in front of an audience, and then posting the videos on the Internet is anything but funny. "Anyway, I swear I'll do *all* the driving when I get my license."

"Don't worry about it, Megan."

"Seriously! I'm gonna do it this time. I signed up for lessons with this new driving school that just opened."

Nicki pushes her long bangs out of her eyes. "I believe you."

I know she's really thinking I'll chicken out like always, but I'm grateful she doesn't say it out loud. She knows that despite the years of therapy, riding in a car still freaks me out.

She takes the turn onto Enchanted Boulevard like a ninety-two-year-old grandmother would, and I point to an office building near the entrance to the park. "The interview is over there."

She pulls into the nearly empty parking lot, which will be jam-packed in a week. "Are you sure you really want to do this?" she asks.

I stare up at the Land of Enchantment sign. Smiling princesses and overly cute forests animals wave their animatronic arms. Even as a kid I wasn't crazy about coming here all that much—the crowds, the two-minute rides that never seemed worth the long wait to get on them. But Remy loved everything about Land of Enchantment, and Dad used to say he'd never seen a pair of twins look at the world so differently.

A small shudder wracks my body. It's been ten years since Remy died, and ten long years of being haunted by her ghost. Coming here is just asking for her to pop up, and I'm wondering if I can pull off an interview with Remy's ghost babbling in the background. I'm very tempted to tell Nicki to put the car in reverse and go home.

But I don't.

"I was getting sick of the bookstore," I lie. "Ever since Diane got promoted to manager, she's been a total bitch. And this way I'll be outside getting a tan instead of spending another summer paler than a vampire."

Nicki shakes her head. "This has nothing to do with getting a tan and you know it. I've kept my mouth shut so far, but to be honest, getting a job here because you're afraid to leave Ryan and Samantha alone is kind of stalkery."

"*Stalkery?* Since when did wanting to spend time with your boyfriend become stalking?"

Nicki gives me an incredulous look.

"Okay! The thought of him and Samantha working together has been driving me nuts, but can you blame me?

She's been his best friend since second grade, and we've only been going out for three weeks and two days."

"This is so not like you! Where's the Megan who'd never chase a guy she just started seeing? Who'd never in a million years *stay* with said guy if she didn't trust him?"

I stare up at the prince on the sign, climbing Rapunzel's long braid. "*That* Megan was tired of not having had a relationship since freshman year. And *that* Megan was confident things were strictly platonic between them until Samantha made one too many trips to the keg and made her 'soul mate' confession. Not to mention the fact that she's totally gorgeous—and nice. How can I compete with that?"

"Yeah, that was *real* nice of her to make a play for Ryan while you were in the bathroom. But despite her drunken confession, he's still with you, so what are you worried about?"

I shrug my shoulders. "I don't know. I just wish he hadn't told me about it."

"He was being honest with you, and if you ask me, that's a good sign."

"Or maybe he was laying the groundwork for our breakup—so it won't come as a big shock when he tells me he's finally realized the girl of his dreams was living right next door all along."

Nicki shakes her head and takes out her iPod. "Good

luck. Hope they assign you to something cool like the hot dog cart. Or if you make a really great impression, maybe they'll give you one of those little brooms and dustpans with the long handles, and you can sweep trash from the walkways."

"Actually it's always been a dream of mine to work the slushy machine, but what I'm really looking forward to is spending the summer endlessly repeating 'Welcome to the Gingerbread Coaster, please keep your hands inside the car until the ride comes to a complete stop.'"

Nicki puts the earbuds in. "I'm gonna listen to some songs; the tryouts are tomorrow and I still haven't decided what to sing." She turns the volume up and I can hear "Defying Gravity" from *Wicked*. "Working at any of the fast-food joints on the outlet strip would be better than this," she says loudly.

I pick up my purse and tell myself I'm above spying on my boyfriend. But then I think about how being with Ryan makes me feel more alive than I have in years, and I open the door and head for the park offices.

I sit in front of Mr. Roy and put on the best I-would-so-be-an-asset-to-your-amusement-park smile I can muster. Looking at his Cinderella tie, I have a feeling he'll be a pushover.

"So . . ." He glances down at my application. "*Megan*, why do you want to work at Land of Enchantment?"

Telling him I've turned into a stalker because good-girl Samantha morphed into a man-stealing bitch is probably not the best approach, so I straighten up, look into his washed-out gray eyes, and lie. "I've loved the Land of Enchantment since I was a little girl, and nothing would make me happier than the opportunity to put a little magic into some kid's summer vacation."

I smile harder and hope I didn't lay it on too thick.

Mr. Roy tilts his head and beams. He clasps his hands under his chin. "Is there a special memory of the park you could share with me? I always love hearing how we've affected people; it's what keeps me going when the day-to-day operation details get overwhelming."

Oh, God, what to pick? Toddler throwing up on the teacup ride? Third-degree sunburns from standing in endless lines? Eating warm egg-salad sandwiches because my parents were too cheap to buy lunch at the park?

"Um, well, I remember this one time, I think I was maybe five, and I was scared to go into Hansel and Gretel's Haunted Forest, and then someone tapped my shoulder. I turned around and there was, uh . . ." My mind scrambles to come up with something plausible. "Uh, there was Snow White. She held out her white-gloved hand and said, 'Don't worry, sweetie; I'll go in with you.' With Snow White by my side, I knew I could do it, and to this day Hansel and Gretel's Haunted Forest is one of my favorite attractions."

Mr. Roy looks teary, and it's all I can do to keep from rolling my eyes. Hansel and Gretel's had to be the lamest thing here—half the animatronics were broken, and the scariest thing about it was that the fact anyone actually paid money to see it.

"Well, Megan, I think we have a spot on our enchanted team for a special girl like you. I see you've checked off ride operations, gift shop, and character actor on your application. I'd bet a bundle you were hoping to fill Snow White's gloves yourself, am I right?" He leans toward me and winks.

Don't-roll-eyes! "Yes, sir, 'Snow White' is one of my favorite stories, and it would be so much fun to play her."

"What a coincidence. 'Snow White' is one of my favorite stories, too. And with your dark hair, you'll be perfect! Unfortunately, you can't be Snow White every day; we try to mix up our team member's experiences so everyone gets a better feel for the park, and we can find those special kids who turn their Land of Enchantment summer jobs into a life-long career. After all, you'd never know whether you have the makings of our future Fun Farm manager if you don't get to spend some time in the Billy Goats

Gruff pen—which we go to great lengths to keep clean."

I smile like this is a wonderful opportunity, all the while praying to God I won't be shoveling crap all summer.

"Your next step is to meet our team coordinator—my wife, Miss Patty."

He winks at me, and I will myself to keep the wide-eyed smiley expression plastered on my face.

"She'll give you our orientation packet and training schedule, and get your size for the costume."

He picks up his phone and pushes a button. "Honey bear, I'm sending a new recruit down." He glances at my application again. "Megan Sones. You'll need to take her to the costume room for a Snow White fitting." He pauses and smiles at me. "She's perfect." He hangs up and pushes his chair away from his desk. "Patty's office is just around the corner. I'll point you in the right direction."

I look around at Miss Patty and her office and I'm thinking she has some unresolved issues that a few years of therapy *might* make a dent in. The walls of her office are bright pink and adorned with portraits of princesses with over-size lightbulb-shaped heads rendered in Day-Glo pastels. PATTY is signed in huge six-inch letters in the bottom right corner of each one, and I wonder how she could've willingly signed her name to these atrocities. Completely out of place with the rest of the décor, a ratty stuffed boar head hangs gathering dust above an overly gilded mirror just behind her desk.

"Megan," Miss Patty says with a hint of a Southern drawl as she extends a well-manicured hand with rings on each finger. "It is such a *pleasure* to meet you! I'm Miss Patty, your enchanted team leader, and it's my job to get you ready for your enchanted summer!"

"Nice to meet you," I say, trying not to stare. High, pointed arcs have been drawn on her forehead way above where her eyebrows should've been, and one of her false eyelashes is crooked. Her face has a brown leathery look to it—like she's spent way too much time in tanning booths—and her curly blond hair extensions don't match the rest of her overly processed, thinning hair.

Miss Patty points to a pink polka-dotted chair and I sit. I look up at the boar's yellowed tusks and ratty fur and can't understand why this woman, who's obviously very concerned with her appearance and the color pink, would have something so totally gross in her office.

"Here's our introduction packet. It has the W-2's and emergency contact forms you'll need to fill out, plus general park information, shift times, and a training schedule. Do you know CPR?"

I nod, picturing myself performing CPR in the Snow

White costume, and wonder if it's too late to run screaming from her office.

"Excellent!" She opens a folder and scribbles something on the paper inside. She looks up at me and flutters her thick eyelashes. "Oh, I would kill for a complexion like yours!"

I hear the door behind me open and turn to see a girl about my age with a thick white-blond ponytail and ice blue eyes. "Patty, Daddy said you had some things for me to file," she says.

Miss Patty frowns. "Ari, can't you see I'm with a new team member?"

Ari stares blankly at her. "I just need the paperwork and I'll be out of your way."

Miss Patty smiles again, but her eyes bulge slightly as if it's taking a great deal of effort to do so. "Megan, this is my daughter, Arianna."

"Hey," Ari says, and she gives me a look like she knows her mom is in serious need of some counseling and/or medication.

"Articulate as ever," Miss Patty mutters.

Ari rolls her eyes and I almost wish I were back with Mr. Roy.

"Nice to meet you," I say, trying to act like there isn't an incredible amount of tension smoldering in the air between Ari and Miss Patty.

"I'm not quite finished with the paperwork, Ari," Miss Patty says. "You'll have to do it tomorrow."

"But I've got auditions tomorrow."

Miss Patty lets out a long sigh. "Auditions are not all day long. Surely you'll find some spare time."

The phone rings, and Miss Patty holds up a finger to me. "Just a second, Megan, honey." She fluffs her hair with her hands, like whoever is on the other end might see her, and then picks up the receiver.

"Yes?" She takes a deep breath as her cheeks redden. "They were supposed to be here a week ago! How are we supposed to serve popcorn without bags? Look, hang on." She pushes a button on the phone. "Ari," she says sweetly. "Would you mind showing Megan where the costume room is and get her dress and shoe size on the Snow White clipboard?"

"Anything to help you out, *Patty*," Ari answers in the same syrupy tone.

Miss Patty picks up the phone again, and Ari tilts her head toward the door.

I take my information packet and follow her out.

"She's my *step*mother," Ari says as soon as she closes the door. "She always forgets to add that part. She thinks just because she married my dad when I was like three that makes her my real mom." Air gives me a sly smile. "It drove her crazy when I started calling her Patty a couple of years ago."

"I'll bet," I say, thinking that if I had a stepmom like that, I might like to stick it to her once in a while too.

"Anyway, she's a complete nut job—her new thing is shaving off her eyebrows so she can pencil them in. She thinks it makes her look like Pamela Anderson."

Knowing how it feels to have a mother who's slightly off, I decide to sacrifice my reputation in hopes of making her feel better. "Well *my* mom dances in competitions with my golden retriever."

Ari's eyes grow wide. "*Seriously?* She dances with your dog?"

"Yup! A fully choreographed, costumed routine. Google 'Fergus and Sally's Fantasy Freestyle' and you can see them in action for yourself. She's recently added footage of their new number, 'Hopelessly Devoted to You,' in which she's wearing a miniskirt she decorated with a BeDazzler."

Ari shakes her head in disbelief. "Wow! I guess both our moms are nutters, then."

I don't say anything and wonder if my mom was always 'nutters' or if it happened after the accident. No. I remember when she and I were close—when she'd let me help her cook. I was Mom's little angel, but now—now I'm nothing.

We walk down the hall, and I look at the old black-and-white photos of the park hanging on the walls. I'm actually impressed they were able to turn what looks like a glorified petting zoo and carousel into the halfway decent amusement park it is today.

Ari turns to me. "So you signed up for Snow White, huh? The bodice is itchy."

"You've been Snow White?"

Ari scoffs. "Patty makes me help out, but I draw the line at walking around the park in character. I've heard some of the girls complain about the costume, though. And here's a tip: If you're posing for a photo op with a family, try to keep the kids between you and the dad. Some of them are horn dogs who'll try to cop a feel while the flash is going off."

"Thanks for the warning," I say, thinking I should beg Diane to give me my job at the bookstore back.

We turn the corner and I gasp. Remy is standing at the end of the hallway, twirling one of her braids in her left hand. She waves. "Meggy," she calls out and starts walking toward us.

I turn to Ari, but she's rattling on about something to do with her stepmother and Botox, oblivious to the fact that my dead twin is heading our way.

I just knew she was going to show up here! Go away, Remy!

"I said this is it."

Ari is pointing to a door label YE OLDE COSTUME SHOPPE. "Oh. Sorry, I, uh, was just thinking about what you said about the dads."

"Don't worry too much about it. The really bad ones tend to gravitate toward the Bo Peep girls. Something about the petticoat—or maybe it's the way they hold the staff that gets their shorts all aflutter."

I smile, but I'm really thinking I need to get out of here. I look past Ari, see the hallway is empty, and exhale. Hopefully Remy just appeared because she likes that I'm at the park, and not because she has something she wants me to see.

Ari opens the door and turns on the light. There are hundreds of brightly colored costumes hanging on rolling stands. "So," Ari says, looking me up and down. "Size six?"

"Eight," I say, wondering if she was just being nice. "And I'm eight in shoes too."

Ari heads to the Snow White rack and pulls out a costume. "Here it is, your golden ticket to playing friend of forest creatures and tiny little men!"

I groan. "Is it too late to cross 'character actor' off my application?"

Ari laughs. "Despite the potential for being groped, wearing a costume is actually a hell of a lot better than being chained to a ride for hours on end. Except for some scheduled stops in the park, you can pretty much do whatever you want. And you're lucky your hair is black. You won't have to wear the wig, which I'd bet sucks when it's ninety degrees out." Ari hangs the costume back up. "Can you sing?"

"God, no! Do I have to?"

"No, but Patty's been talking about maybe having a character sing-along."

"Yeah, I think my voice would clear the park, but my best friend sings. She's in the White Mountain Chorus. Actually, she's waiting for me, so I should—"

Ari's mouth drops open. "I'm in the chorus too! Well, I was last year, and I'm trying out again tomorrow. Who's your friend?"

"Nicki Summers, and like I said, she's waiting—"

Ari claps her hands. "Oh my God, I know Nicki! She has an *amazing* voice; she kept beating me out for solos. I can't even believe they're making her try out. I mean, everyone knows she's gonna make it. So she's here?"

"Yeah, she's in the parking lot, but Nicki told me the old director left, so everyone's starting from scratch this year."

"Huh, I didn't know Mr. Sherman left. Of course he would've told Nicki—they were tight." Ari starts stalking around the costume rack. "I'd love to find out what she's singing. Let me put your info on the clipboard, and then I'll go out with you." She shakes her head. "Damn, it's not here. *Patty* probably left it in the laundry room. Let me run down and see if I can find it. Hold on."

As soon as Ari leaves, the temperature in the room rapidly drops. "Remy," I say, my breath frosting in the air. "I don't want to play with you." The lights flicker and a cold sweat breaks out on my forehead.

"Meeeeggy." Her voice echoes in my head. "I have something to show you."

I back up toward the door, legs trembling, and scan the room for Remy. "I don't *like* the things you show me, Remy."

The door slams shut behind me and I jump. "Fine! What is it?" I yell, sounding braver than I feel. I learned long ago that trying to ignore Remy just pisses her off, and I should get this over with before she starts throwing things.

Remy appears by the Snow White rack. Water drips to the floor from the hem of her dress and the tips of her braids. She frowns and beckons to me with her small seven-year-old hand. "Meggy, come see."

"What? The costumes?" I picture trying on clothes from the dress-up box Grammy gave us when we were five, and a tear rolls down my cheek. "I'm gonna play dress-up this summer, Remy—as Snow White." I point to the costumes and hope I can divert her attention from whatever it is she wants to show me. "Do you wanna see me put one on?"

Remy nods and puts the end of one of her braids in her mouth, and I remember how Mom used to dip the tips in Tabasco sauce, trying to break her of the habit.

I walk slowly toward her, and she points to a costume in the middle of the rack.

As I reach out for the satin sleeve, Remy touches my arm. An icy chill runs through me, and the room disappears. I see a girl wearing a Snow White costume lying on the ground in a wooded area. It's dark, and I squint at the black stain on her bodice. I bend down and realize the bodice is unlaced, and while the blouse is soaked in what I think is blood, the darkest stain is actually a hole—a hole in her chest cavity where her heart should've been.

"Be careful, Meggy," Remy whispers as everything goes black.

∽ TWO ∽

"Hey, are you all right? Can you hear me?"

I feel hands gently shaking my shoulders. I open my eyes and see I'm lying on the floor of the costume room. A guy about my age with dark, worried eyes is kneeling beside me. I reach up and my fingers automatically flutter across my chest like they were expecting to find a hole.

"Yeah, I think so." I push myself up and wince as a sharp pain stabs the back of my head. "Ow," I groan, touching the egg-size lump.

"Maybe you'd better stay down. I'll get Patty."

"No, it's okay. I just fainted. I do that sometimes."

He reaches out and I let him help me up. His hand feels warm, and I'm so cold, I almost don't want to let it go. He runs his fingers though his curly black hair and stares at me like he's afraid I'll pass out again. "I was heading to the woodshop when I heard you scream."

My cheeks flush. "I didn't know I screamed, but it was nothing. I thought I saw a, uh, mouse."

"Oh," he says, eyebrows raised. "I figured it had something to do with your sister."

My heart races as my eyes flash to the spot where Remy was, but there's only a small puddle of water on the floor. I swallow hard and turn back to him. "You—you saw her?"

He holds up a hand just below his chest. "About this tall, dark braids, freckles?"

"Uh-huh," I squeak out, both stunned and relieved that someone else has seen her.

"She said her name is Remy and she asked me to tell you she's sorry."

"She *talked* to you?"

He nods. "It's no big deal really. I'm kind of a ghost magnet—runs in the family. Remy is the forty-seventh one I've met. Well, the forty-seventh since I started keeping track in second grade. But besides introducing herself, she told me your name is Megan, she hates peas, and she's pretty bummed her cat was hit by a car."

"Wow," I whisper. "I don't get that much out of her. I mean, she talks, but a lot of the time it's incoherent . . ." I pause, trying to get the image of the girl in the Snow White costume out of my head. "Unless she wants to show me something—usually something bad."

"Did she show you something *here*?" he asks, worry furrowing his brow. "Is that what she was she apologizing for? What did you see?"

He looks at me expectantly. I move closer to him, not sure I can actually say it out loud. "Uh, yeah. She, uh—"

"It *was* in the laundry, but I put your name down and . . ." Ari is saying as she enters the room. She pauses when she sees I'm not alone. "Luke, what're you doing here?" She looks back and forth between us and frowns.

Luke takes a step away from me and runs a hand through his dark hair again. "Hey, Ari. I was just passing by on my way to the shop when I heard someone in here. I thought maybe it was you and I came in to say hello."

"Oh," Ari says brightly. She hangs the clipboard on the Snow White rack and smiles at him. "So you've met Megan, one of our drones, I mean *enchanted team members*."

Luke gives me a military salute. "As one drone to another, welcome aboard."

Ari walks over to him and links an arm with his. At first I think they might be going out, but then he pulls away from her slightly, so maybe I'm wrong.

"You won't see Luke out in the park too often," she

says. "He spends most of his time in the shop down the hall squandering his talents."

"I'll have you know, Ari," Luke starts as he gently unhooks himself from her and folds his arms across his chest, "that your dad got all teary eyed when he saw my Sleeping Beauty mural on the wall leading up to the girls' bathrooms in the Fairy Tale Forest. And your mom went *nuts* for the brick and vine work I added to Rapunzel's tower—she took about fifty pictures of it and compared me to da Vinci."

Ari scoffs. "Not counting the fact that Patty *is* nuts, I'd reserve the da Vinci comparison to the stuff you did *before* you started painting plywood murals that people stick their used gum on."

Luke bites his lip and hugs his arms tighter. Obviously, Ari hit a sore spot. "Hey, at least your parents appreciate what I'm doing."

Ari looks at him defiantly. "*I* appreciate what you're doing too, but I'm not gonna let you forget that you're too good to be decorating the bathrooms!"

"Gum-covered princesses are about all I can handle right now," he says. "I thought you, of all people, would understand."

Ari puts her hands on her hips. "*Luke!* I—"

Luke turns to me, ignoring her. "Nice to meet you, Megan. We should *definitely* finish our conversation sometime soon."

He leaves, and Ari stares after him, her cheeks a fiery red. "God, he can be *so* impossible!" A shudder runs through her like she's trying to shake him off. "Anyway, we have black shoes that we'll set aside for you, but they're kind of gross, so if you have a pair, I'd bring them. Your costume will have your name pinned to it, and there'll be a ribbon for your hair too. Come on, I'll walk you out."

I follow Ari into the hallway, thinking this day has been a little too surreal and I should go and tell Miss Patty to rip up my application. But Luke saw Remy. He talked to her! Despite the weirdness, maybe there's a reason I came here— maybe he can help me.

Of course, there is the *little* issue of the dead girl I saw. I try to conjure her face, but I was so focused on the hole in her chest, I didn't look at her carefully. But the million-dollar question is: Was that something that *did* happen, or something that *will* happen?

You never know with Remy. She showed me a vision of Grandma Miller collapsing in her hospital room hours before the blood clot lodged in her brain and killed her. But our cat Pumpkin had been missing for two days before Remy dropped the catnip mouse on my pillow in the middle of the night and showed me his body flattened on the road a few blocks away.

Ari stops in front of a painting and waves her hand dismissively at the princess with large emerald eyes surrounded by butterflies. "This is one of Luke's *new* paintings." She shakes her head. "I've got a bunch of his old pieces in my room. I'll show you, and then you tell me if you think he should be holed up here working on fairy-tale floozies!"

"Uh, okay," I say, thinking Luke's painting is a gazillion times better than the stuff hanging in her stepmother's office and wondering if she's implying that she's going to invite me over to her house. We walk toward the front entrance and I wonder if Ari lives in the Tudor mansion up on the mountain above the park.

"He lives with his grandmother," she continues, "but she's too busy scamming tourists with her tarot cards and crystal crap that she doesn't care he's totally blowing it." She shakes her head again and scowls. "Have you seen that purple house at the end of the outlet strip?" she asks.

"Yeah, it's kinda hard to miss," I say. You can't go into town without driving by the lilac Victorian with the AMADOR'S PSYCHIC READINGS sign sitting in an overgrown yard filled with hundreds of lawn ornaments.

I've been tempted to go there on more than one occasion, hoping they could help me with Remy—help her move on to wherever it is she should've gone. But when I asked Nicki a few years ago if she thought they were legit, she laughed so hard she spewed the lemon water she was drinking across her kitchen table. When she finally got herself together, she said that anyone with more than twenty lawn gnomes in their yard was most definitely a psycho, not a psychic.

"Well, that's Luke's house, if you can believe it," Ari says, wrinkling her nose. "And his grandmother is too wrapped up reading tea leaves to notice that's he's given up painting!"

"Well, technically he is still painting," I say, not sure why I'm feeling an overpowering urge to stick up for him. "Maybe this is just what he needs to be doing right now— you know, like Picasso had his blue period; maybe this is Luke's plywood period."

Ari throws her hands up—my attempt at lightening the mood is obviously a bust. "Oh, please! Do you really consider Sleeping Beauty laid out snoring by the crapper *art*?"

"I guess not, but I did see Rapunzel's tower on my way in; it *was* really good," I add, knowing I'm pushing it, as she's made it abundantly clear Luke Amador is a subject she's very passionate about.

She turns to me with narrowed eyes.

Here it comes.

"Luke isn't just 'really good.' Luke is someday-people-will-pay-big-bucks-for-his-work amazing. *If* I can get him out of this freaking park! I told my dad not to hire him, but everyone felt so bad for him after his sister disappeared last . . ." Ari pauses like she's suddenly realized she's said too much.

"Was that Luke's sister on the posters that were up last summer?" I ask. "The girl with blond hair like yours?" She didn't go to my school so at the time I didn't give it much thought. I certainly didn't think she'd still be missing a year later, though.

Ari nods. "They never found her, and he took it hard."

"Yeah, I bet he did." I know firsthand how hard losing a sister is. "Do they have any clues or leads?"

"Nothing. She disappeared without a trace. But maybe you're right, maybe this is what he needs to be doing—for now."

Ari starts walking quickly down the hall, and I rush to keep up with her. She gives me a quick look. "So what were you and Luke talking about before? It looked like I interrupted a *moment*."

Ah, now I get it. Ari has it bad for Luke, the feeling isn't mutual, and she's worried I was moving in on him. Given my own boyfriend troubles, I'd laugh out loud if it wasn't for the fact that the "moment" she interrupted was preceded by a vision of some girl splayed out on the ground with her heart inexplicably missing. But I've had years of practice keeping my emotions in check and pretending everything's okay, so I easily push the image out of my head and carry on.

"Oh, he was just asking me what brought me to the Land of Enchantment. I was trying to decide if I should admit I'm here so I can keep an eye on my boyfriend and his best friend, *Samantha*."

After all the lies I've told today, it feels good that this is at least a half truth.

Ari's shoulders relax, and I figure she's relieved to hear that not only do I have a boyfriend but also I can relate to how she's feeling.

"Samantha?"

"Yeah, Samantha—an overly perky, four-foot-eleven, sports-loving cheerleader who recently told my boyfriend she thinks he's her soul mate. Couple the confession with the fact that they spend just about all their free time together and I'm feeling a little paranoid."

"Oh my God! What kind of a person does that?" Ari asks, a look of outrage on her face.

"*Samantha Lee Darling* does. Well, after a few too many beers, that is."

"Ew, even her name is perky! You just say the word and I'll make sure they're working at opposite ends of the park all summer. Or"—she gives me a sly smile—"I can go one better and have her assigned to the rides most likely to induce vomiting. Mopping up puke all day will definitely take the perky factor down a few notches."

As much as I want to take her up on the offer, I decide to at least pretend I've still got some dignity. "Thanks, but you know what? If my being here isn't going to stop them from hooking up, nothing will, right?"

"I guess, but I bet you can hold your own against Miss Perky."

A clap of thunder shakes the windows and I jump. We near the doors to the parking lot just as the rain hits full force. Nicki would never make me ride in a car during a storm like this, but the airways in my lungs start to constrict just seeing the water pooling around her car. The clouds are whipping by at top speed. These storms never last long, but I know how dangerous they can be.

"Shit," Ari says. "Let's wait a few minutes until it passes."

I nod and reach into my purse for my inhaler.

Ari's phone starts playing "When You Wish Upon a Star." She takes it out of the holster clipped to her belt and scowls. "Damn, it's Patty." She hits a button and puts it up to her ear. "Yeah?" She shakes her head and exhales loudly. "I thought you said you wouldn't have it done until tomorrow. Well, I'm doing something now." Ari rolls her eyes. "No, you don't have to call Daddy. I'll do it!"

She hangs up and groans. "'I guess I'll just have to call your father and have him tell payroll to cancel this week's check since you're too busy doing nothing to earn it,'" she says, doing a dead-on imitation of her stepmother. "I could kill my father for marrying that witch and making my life a living hell! The summer I was ten she made me scrub toilets in the park so I could learn to 'appreciate' all the employees' hard work! Do you know many toilets we have?"

"Uh, a lot?"

"*Sixty-five* and I've cleaned each and every one of them." She hands me her phone. "Put your number in. I'll give you a call tonight and you can tell me what Nicki's singing, okay?"

"Okay," I say, punching it in, "but sometimes she doesn't pick a song until the last minute."

"Maybe you guys can come over sometime. I go to White Cliff Academy and most of my friends—besides Luke—summer elsewhere, so I'm stuck here in la-la land with nothing to do but obey Patty's every command."

"Sure, that'd be great," I say, thinking Luke's family must be raking in the dough reading tarot cards if they can afford to send him to White Cliff.

Ari's phone starts playing "When You Wish Upon a Star" again. "Oh my freaking God," she mutters as she takes it from me. She pushes a button and yells, "I'm coming already!" She rolls her eyes as she clicks the phone off and shoves it back into its holster. "I'll call you."

"Great."

She turns the corner, and I take a hit of my inhaler. I count to ten and exhale as I open the door to the parking lot. Running toward Nicki's car I wonder how long it'll take me to bike from my house to Luke's so we can finish our conversation.

THREE

Slamming the car door shut, I'm relieved to see Nicki's taken the keys out of the ignition and left them on the dashboard—her way of letting me know she'll wait for me to say when it's time to leave.

"Well?" Nicki says as she turns her off iPod. "Are you gainfully employed?"

I hold up my information packet. "Yup, and I met a friend of yours."

Nicki raises one eyebrow. "Oh?"

"Arianna Roy."

"Ari Roy works *here*?" She shakes her head. "I never in a million years would've thought she'd be slumming it in the Land of Misogyny."

"Oh, please!"

"Sorry," she continues. "Land of Enchantment isn't just about stereotypically helpless women in need of rescue—there's Hansel and Gretel's Haunted Forest, which is more of a celebration of child abuse and cannibalism, and the petting zoo in Mother Goose's Family Fun Farm, which is all E. coli, all the time!"

I have to laugh. Nicki has never gotten over falling into a huge pile of crap at the Fun Farm during her first and last visit to the park when she was four. "Actually, according to Ari's father—*the owner of the park*—they take great pride in the sanitary conditions at the farm, which I sincerely hope I'm never assigned to work at. I don't care how fast the poop is scooped, when it's ninety-five degrees out, that goat and pig crap is gonna smell worse than the rotting pile of gym clothes and half-eaten sandwiches lying at the bottom of Cooper Summerfield's locker!"

Nicki waves her hand in front of her nose. "Oh, God, I'm having an olfactory flashback to last Friday. Figures our lockers get the afternoon sun—all that sweat and stink just marinates in the heat. Who knows what exciting odor du jour Cooper will subject us to senior year?" She shakes her fist in the air. "Damn you alphabetical order."

Blue sky shows through some of the clouds shredding in the wind, and I hand Nicki her keys. "Maybe we could sneak one of those air sanitizers into his locker," I say as I pull the seat belt across my chest.

Nicki starts the ignition and backs up. "I still can't believe Ari kept quiet about the fact that she's the heir to the Land of Enchantment for the two years we've been in the chorus. Not that we talk too often—Ari's a little too hot and cold for me, so I try to avoid her."

I nod. "Yeah, I experienced some of Ari's many moods today, but you know, she's had a rough life."

"Rough life? Her dad owns a freaking amusement park—which explains why she goes to White Cliff and drives a Mercedes!"

"Uh, if money equaled happy, the rehabs in Hollywood would be out of business. And anyway, would *you* be bragging about being the heir apparent to the Land of Enchantment?"

"No!"

"See? And she's got a father who, in my opinion, has an extremely unhealthy obsession with fairy tales. Add a wacko stepmother to the mix and I think a *rough life* applies."

Nicki tilts her head from side to side as if considering whether she thinks Ari has racked up enough teen angst points to agree with me. "I guess. And it couldn't have been easy after Kayla checked out."

"Huh?"

"Kayla was in the chorus—decent alto—she was Ari's BFF until she went missing last year."

"Oh my God," I say slowly. "I think I met Kayla's brother at the park today."

"Hot guy—curly black hair, fabulous biceps?"

I nod. "That's Luke."

"He used to pick them up after practice sometimes," she says as a smile breaks out on her face. "He's got the dark, brooding thing down pat, that's for damn sure."

"Yes, he does," I say with a little too much enthusiasm.

Nicki gives me a quick look, and my cheeks flush. I turn away from her to watch the scenery out the window.

"Is someone forgetting she has a boyfriend?"

"Since when does having a boyfriend mean you can't appreciate a good-looking guy?"

"It doesn't, but the way Ari was always hanging on him, I wouldn't be surprised if she's had her name forcibly tattooed on his ass. If you want to keep your *fabulous* new job, I'd be careful about admiring him so openly."

A shiver runs through me as Remy's "Be careful, Meggy" echoes in my head. "Um," I choke out, "don't worry about it. Ari's pretty much guaranteed that Ryan and I will be working side by side with no Luke in sight."

I decide not to tell Nicki I'm planning to visit Luke the first chance I get. She's 100 percent grounded in a reality that isn't haunted by ghosts. There's no way she'd believe I just want to see Luke to talk about my dead sister and the Stephen King–like vision she showed me.

I look back out the window and roll my eyes. Not only does Nicki not believe in ghosts but in second grade, after I told her about Remy coming back, she went home and told her mom, who told *my* mom. That got me four months of drawing pictures of my family with my stupid therapist until she was convinced I'd faced the truth about what happened to Remy and Dad.

Like their empty places at the kitchen table didn't scream the truth every day.

At least Nicki was apologetic. Mom just increased my visits to Dr. Macardo and checked out of my life a little bit more. Talk about needing therapy.

"So what was Kayla like?" I ask, hoping to change the subject.

"She was nice, kind of quiet." Nicki shrugs. "She let Ari do most of the talking. They did have a couple of catfights, which I attributed to Ari being genetically predisposed to bitchiness. The weird thing was that shortly after Kayla went missing, Ari showed up at practice with her hair bleached just like Kayla's."

"Seriously?"

"Yeah, until then Ari's hair was closer to your color. At least she's got the money to maintain it. You know how much it drives me crazy when people let their roots get out of control. I did overhear a couple of the older chorus members saying it was probably Ari's way of keeping Kayla's memory alive, but I never bought that. I just think something about her is off."

"Well, you probably won't be too psyched to hear she wants to hang out with us this summer. She's also planning on calling me tonight to find out what you're singing for the audition."

"Oh, God. Don't get involved with her, Meg, our lives have enough drama."

"It might be fun to see how the Mercedes crowd lives, and it's not like I'll be able to avoid her at the park."

"Whatever, just leave me out of the equation, okay?"

We turn the corner onto my street and I see Mom's car in the driveway. "Do you want to come in and see how the new routine went?"

Nicki shakes her head as she parks in front of my house. "I should practice my song. Tell your new BFF I'm singing 'Moments in the Woods.'"

"Ari was surprised to hear you were actually practicing. She said you're a shoo-in."

"Well, that was surprisingly nice of her to say, but with the new director you never know how it'll go—I don't want to get cocky."

"Hey, I'm bringing Ryan to visit my dad this afternoon."

She raises her eyebrows. "Really?"

"I know we haven't been going out that long, but Ryan asked about him—something Jason *never* did the entire six months we were together. Anyway, it's Fergus's therapy dog visit today at the nursing home, so I asked Ryan if he wanted to go. I made it sound like it was more about entertaining the residents—something he can get service hours for—and then I casually mentioned he could meet my dad too." I smile. "He said he'd love to meet him."

"That's cool," Nicki says. "And God knows those little old ladies will *love* having Ryan there."

"That reminds me. Mr. Archulata keeps asking when you're coming back."

Nicki snorts. "The guy who felt me up? He's the reason I'm staying away!"

I laugh. "Well, maybe he was looking for something a little more exciting than dragging his oxygen tank around."

She shakes her head. "I'll come with you next month, but this time *you* can sit with him and listen to his endless war stories."

I open the car door. "It's a deal! Good luck tomorrow, and thanks for the ride."

Nicki waves as she pulls away. I head up the front porch and hear Olivia Newton-John's "Hopelessly Devoted to

You" coming from the open basement window. Poor Fergus. If Mom's putting him through his paces right after the competition, it means the new routine wasn't as ready as she'd hoped.

I grab a dog biscuit from the bowl on the kitchen counter and walk down the basement stairs. Mom's still in costume, and she's singing along to the CD. Fergus has his eyes glued to her, watching for hand commands. She turns to the slow beat of the song and twirls her finger in the air.

"No, spin!" Mom yells as Fergus rolls on his back.

"Fergie!" I call out. Fergus freezes for a second, and then hops up and runs over to me. I make a fist and he sits. "Say hello."

Fergus sneezes and then gives me a deep, gravelly Scooby-Doo "Rello."

I toss him the biscuit and turn to see Mom staring at me, hands on her hips, obviously pissed I've interrupted them.

"Didn't go well?" I ask.

Mom shakes her head and turns off the CD. "Second place! I shouldn't have tried something so new for the competition."

"Second place is still pretty good."

She looks at me like I've just said something completely scandalous. "Good? I haven't had a second place showing in over a year! And the first-place winner came out of nowhere—some balding man with a horrific Brussels griffon dancing to 'Love Shack,' of all things. If he's going to be a regular on the competition circuit, I've got to step up my game." Mom wrinkles her nose. "You should've seen Kathy Gates acting all smug because someone finally beat us."

"Is she the lady with the really bad perm and the Labradoodle?

"Yes, she rarely cracks the top five with the tired routine she's been sleepwalking through the last three years! I should've at least gotten some points for trying something new."

I sit down on the floor. Fergus cuddles up to me and puts his head in my lap. "Maybe you need to pick something up-tempo," I say, hoping she'll choose a new song.

She adjusts her skirt and I try not to cringe. It's way too short for a forty-seven-year-old who needs to lose fifteen pounds. "We just need to work a little harder, that's all. But we'll have this nailed by the next competition!"

I count to five hoping she'll ask me about the job interview.

"Well, why don't you head up so we can keep practicing? You know Fergus can't concentrate if he thinks you'll be throwing him biscuits all the time."

"I got the job, in case you were wondering."

She gives me a blank look. "You already have a job."

"I quit the bookstore, remember? So Nicki took me to Land of Enchantment for an interview." I rub Fergus's velvety ears, knowing she'll never admit she was only half-listening to me yesterday morning when I asked her for a ride.

She unties the scarf wrapped around her ponytail and shakes her graying hair out around her shoulders. "Oh, right. I guess I forgot it was today."

That's because all you care about is the dog, I'm tempted to say. "You did remember I'm taking Fergus to see Dad this afternoon, right?"

"Of course I remember," she says, but I'm not convinced.

"I'm bringing Ryan too."

"Tell your father I'll be by tomorrow, okay?"

"Sure." I wait, hoping she'll note that I must be really serious about Ryan because I've never taken anyone but Nicki to see Dad. Or maybe she'll mention that I should invite him over for dinner so she can get to know him better.

Something. Anything.

"Fergus, come!" she commands.

He pops up and stands at her side. "Can you push the play button before you go?"

"Sure," I say again. "Don't tire him out too much; he's not as young as he used to be and Dad's roommate likes to see him do tricks." I turn on the CD and walk up the stairs.

That's the longest conversation we've had in weeks.

* * *

"Thanks for letting me come," Samantha chirps as she skips ahead of Ryan and me on the walkway to the nursing home. Her long, blond pigtails swish back and forth, and I roll my eyes—only she could get away with wearing pigtails after the age of ten. "I *really* need to knock some time off my community involvement hours. I still have like twenty-one to go."

I shrug. "No problem." *Given the fact you were already in the car when Ryan picked me up, what choice did I have?*

With great effort I maintain my smile to mask the bitterness eating at my gut. I know *part* of this is my fault. I should've let Ryan know I don't bring just anyone to see Dad, but still.

At least Ryan seemed genuinely psyched to hear about my new Land of Enchantment gig. And getting to see Samantha's jaw drop when I shared the news almost made it worth having her here.

Almost.

Ryan squeezes my hand and I look up at him. He gives me the same soulful "I'm sorry" look he had on his face when I saw Samantha waving from the front seat of his car.

"She really wanted to come when I told her about this," he said in a hushed voice on the front steps of my house. "I felt bad saying no because she's been all freaked out about getting her hours done for graduation."

"She still has all of senior year," I said.

Ryan's shoulders slumped and he squeezed his green eyes shut for a second. "I know. And I know I need to talk to her about giving us some more space, and I will. She just doesn't have a lot of other friends, and she's used to doing everything with me. But I'll talk to her. I promise."

"Whatever."

He wrapped his arms around me and pulled me close. "You're the best," he whispered. "And I'll make it up to you; dinner and a movie tonight—just us—and we can make plans for our next hike."

A real smile comes to my lips at the thought. And at least he made her get in the backseat with Fergus, who never fails to drool copiously during car rides.

We get to the entrance and Fergus sits as the doors slide open. "He's waiting for the okay to go in," I explain as the overly warm nursing-home air—smelling of a mix of disinfectant and urine—rushes out and hits me in the face.

Samantha elbows Ryan. "Awww, isn't that cute? I should've brought Muffin."

"Oh, please. There is absolutely nothing therapeutic about Muffin," I snap. "And you can't bring just any dog into a nursing home. You'd have to have him certified as a therapy dog, which involves a test of basic manners and commands, which, I might add, Muffin is sorely lacking!"

I shake my head. The thought of that fifteen-pound nightmare cutting it as a therapy dog is laughable.

Of course, my plan to get Fergus certified so I could try to reconnect with Mom is laughable too. I'd hoped if I was involved with the only thing she showed any real interest in—Fergus—she might remember there was someone who survived the accident intact. Instead of suggesting we work on it together, she worried that new training might affect their freestyle routines. God forbid!

I realize no one is talking and turn to see Ryan and a wounded-looking Samantha staring at me. "I have read that Jack Russell terriers are one of *the* toughest breeds to train, though," I say, trying to do some damage control.

"Yeah," she says softly. "I've read that too."

Ryan puts an arm around my shoulders and I relax. "And, Sammy," he says, "Muffin barks at anything that moves. He'd set off a string of cardiac arrests if you brought him in."

She pouts at Ryan. "Muffin's not *that* bad."

I'm tempted to say, *She sure as hell is that bad,* but I think I've played the shrew card enough for one day.

"Okay, Fergus," I say, and we step onto the welcome mat. The receptionist, Mary, looks up from her laptop and waves.

"Here's my two favorite visitors," she says. "With reinforcements!"

"Hi, Mary," I say as I sign in. "This is my boyfriend, Ryan, and his neighbor Samantha. They're going to work on some of their service hours."

"Nice to meet you," Mary says. "We always love visitors."

Ryan signs in and then reaches for my hand and gives it a squeeze. "And I finally get to meet Mr. Sones!"

"Oh yeah, Ryan told me your dad works here," Samantha says, looking around like my dad might be wandering around in a white coat, waving at us.

Mary quickly turns away to get our visitor tags, and I shake my head. "My dad's a *resident* here. He has been for the last ten years. He never woke up after a car accident."

Samantha's jaw drops for the second time today as she glares at Ryan. "Why didn't you tell me?"

Ryan looks at me with panic in his eyes. "I didn't say he worked here, I said he *was* here." He turns to Samantha. "I thought you knew about Megan's dad."

"How would I know about her dad?"

"Ryan," I say, "Samantha didn't move here until *after* the accident."

"Oh, shit," he says, and then his eyes flash to Mary. "Sorry, Miss—uh, Mary!" He rubs his hand nervously across his jaw. "I'm such an idiot."

Samantha starts to back away. "I am *so* sorry, Megan, I thought this was just about getting hours! I never would have come along if I knew you were bringing him here to meet your father. Why don't I go and wait in the car."

I reach out and touch her hand. "Don't go. A lot of the people here never get any visitors; they'd be really disappointed if you left. And Mr. Archulata on the second floor keeps asking me when I'm gonna leave Fergus home and bring him some hot chicks."

She gives me a half smile. "Okay, but I wish Ryan had told me," she says as she swats him on the arm.

I smile back at her, thinking that even though it's hard to hate her sometimes, I'm not going to warn her about Mr. Archulata and his wandering hands.

"Megan," Mary says as she hands us our tags. "Mr. Peck passed away on Tuesday."

I sigh. I've lost track of how many roommates Dad's had. They keep dying while he lingers on and on, thanks to a feeding tube.

I push away the thought that they're the lucky ones.

"He was my dad's latest roommate," I say finally.

Mr. Peck loved having Fergus jump up into bed with him. He'd stroke his fur and tell me about all the dogs he'd had. I heard the same stories so many times, I'm sure I could repeat them verbatim. "Thanks for the heads-up, Mary."

I straighten Fergus's therapy-dog bandanna and tilt my head toward the meeting room. "We'll start down here—

there'll be a bunch of people who always like to get out of their rooms to see Fergus do his tricks, and then we can split up or you can come with me while we visit some of the people who aren't mobile."

Ryan and Samantha nod, but from their pale faces, I'm guessing neither of them is ready to strike out on their own. I don't blame them—being surrounded by people on the verge of dying is a scary thing.

Ryan and I leave Samantha in the hall with Mr. Archulata and head to Dad's room. I open the door and take in Mr. Peck's stripped-down bed. Fergus sniffs it on his way over to Dad and then he sits while I pull a chair up next to his bed. Fergus jumps up, puts his paws on the side rail. He drops his head gently across Dad's chest, which is moving up and down slowly—his exhalations sounding wheezy and labored. I make a note to tell the nurse so they can keep an eye on him in case he might be developing pneumonia. I pick up Dad's left arm and drape it gently over Fergus.

Suddenly, Remy appears, wispy and unfocused on the other side of the bed. She flickers in and out view, twisting and wringing her braids.

What is going on? Besides the fact that she's never shown up at the nursing home before, I can't remember a time when she's shown up twice in one day! I've always counted on getting at least a month or so reprieve between visits, which keeps me from going crazy.

Remy walks toward the window and disappears. *"Star light, star bright, first star I see tonight."* Her voice echoes around the room.

I purse my lips. Remy and I used to sit on the back deck and scan the sky at dusk for the first evening star; as soon as one of us spotted it, we'd race through that poem—each of us hoping to finish first and claim the wish.

Ryan shuffles his feet next to me and I know I should say something, but I'm frozen in place as I listen to Remy's singsong words.

"I wish I may, I wish I might, have the wish I wish tonight."

She appears again by my side and I catch my breath as her icy ghost hand reaches out for mine.

I need to block her out. I can't let on that anything is wrong.

She starts the rhyme again and I study Dad's sunken face and the dark stubble on his cheeks and chin. The nurses usually give him a shave when they know I'm coming in, but maybe there were more pressing things to take care of today. Tears well up in my eyes as I visually trace the length of his arm—atrophied from lack of use—as it hangs limply on Fergus.

Persistent vegetative state.

"I wish I may, I wish I might, have the wish I wish tonight."

My heart sinks as Remy's words drive home what I've avoided thinking about all these years—that deep down I've always known that what the doctors have been telling us was true, and the miraculous recovery we've been wishing for is never going to happen. This shell of a person lying in the bed is not my father, and no matter how many times we come here and try to bring him back with our touch, our voices, or even Fergus, no matter how many times we've wished for it, he's never waking up.

"Meg?" Ryan whispers.

He threads an arm around my waist, and Remy vanishes again. He draws me close to him. His touch warms me and I realize I'm shivering.

I try to remember how it felt to be in Dad's arms.

I can't.

"Meg? Are you going to introduce me?"

"No." Tears finally overflow and stream down my cheeks. "No, there's no point."

Remy solidifies in front of me, her panicked eyes locked onto mine. She's so clear I can see each and every freckle on her nose. "Meggy, where's Daddy?" she says, her voice quavering.

I shudder as my body grows colder. "He's right here," I whisper.

"What?" Ryan asks.

Remy balls her hands into fists, and water sprays out as they shake at her side. "Where is he, Meggy? I'm so scared and I don't know how to help you."

The lightbulbs on the bedside tables pop, sending a shower of glass and sparks cascading down. Dad's monitor sputters and smokes, and an alarm sounds.

"Where's Daddy?" she screams.

"Oh my God. We have to get out of here. Fergus! Come!" I pull on Ryan's arm and drag him out of the room.

"Where do we get help?" he asks, looking wildly around the hall.

"They'll hear the alarm," I say, gasping for breath.

Remy's shrieks echo in the hallway. *"Daddy! Help me! Daddy!"*

Nurses run toward us as I fumble in my purse for my inhaler.

"Meg, it's going to be okay," he says, reaching out for me.

"No, it's not—Remy's getting worse."

∽ FOUR ∽

I lie on the couch with a blanket drawn up to my chin to ward off the cold Remy brought with her. Fergus is curled up at my feet, his eyes tracking Remy as she paces back and forth in front of the TV. At least she's transparent right now, so she's not blocking my view. Not that I can really pay attention when she's muttering to herself like this.

Fergus lets out a series of whimpers, hops down to the floor, and trots off to the kitchen.

"Are you happy? You scared the dog!" I yell at her.

I throw a pillow at her, but she doesn't miss a stride and continues looking aimlessly around the room. "Bad. Bad. Gotta find Daddy. Daddy will know what to do. I don't know. I don't know."

"Dad's in the nursing home. Don't you remember, you destroyed some very expensive monitors in his room today?"

Remy keeps pacing and I shake my head, wondering when Mom will get back from the nursing home. No doubt she's ripped the director a new one for not being able to explain Remy's pyrotechnic display this afternoon. I feel bad for the guy—it's not his fault Remy went bonkers. And from past experience I know no electrician in the world would be able to explain the spontaneous blowup.

Of course, also based on past experience, Mom should put two and two together and recall that exploding lightbulbs and faulty electronics have been a fairly normal occurrence at our house since the accident. Maybe she'll even remember I told her years ago it was Remy who was causing all the trouble—before I adopted her "sane" explanation about the lighting industry bilking consumers by making shoddy products. Of course, I would've agreed to just about anything to avoid extra sessions with Dr. Macardo.

I shake my head. It was bloody brilliant of me to mention Remy's name at the nursing home. Ryan probably thinks I'm some sort of freak now. "If he breaks up with me, it's all your fault!"

"Bad. Bad. I don't know. Star light, star bright—"

"Shut up!" I scream.

Remy stops suddenly and jerks her head toward me. She

solidifies and the temperature in the room dips even more. "Meggy!"

I roll my eyes. Nice going. I *had* to get her attention.

Remy walks toward me and gives me a crooked smile. I watch a drip roll down her forehead and hang for a second at the end of her nose. I listen to the sound of the river pounding against the car so many years ago. "That boy can help."

"Luke?"

The doorbell rings and Remy laughs. "I wish I may, I wish I might," she says as she turns and skips away, fading as she goes.

I shudder uncontrollably as I pull the blanket off. "Uh, I'm coming."

I look out the window and see Ryan's car parked at the curb. Did Remy know Ryan was there? Is that who she meant? I open the door and he's holding a large brown bag with a Chinese menu stapled to the top and several DVDs.

"Since you said you weren't up for going out tonight, I thought I'd bring the food and entertainment to you."

He gives me a wide-eyed, hopeful look, and just seeing his green eyes chases the cold from me. I lean in and kiss him. "You're the best."

He smiles. "I'm trying, and I hope this helps make up for that boneheaded move I pulled earlier with Sammy."

I nod as I lead him in. "This definitely helps."

I take the food and put it on the coffee table.

"Wow, it's cold in here," he says as he sits on the couch.

"Uh, my mom had the AC cranked up. I just lowered it, though." I do a quick scan of the room and see Remy standing at the window, her back to us. I wonder if Ryan will mention how cold Dad's room got before the fireworks started, but if he's anything like Mom, he won't. No one seems capable of connecting the dots.

I sit next to Ryan and he wraps an arm around me. "I'll keep you warm."

I lean into him and breathe in his freshly showered, soapy smell. He kisses my cheek and then traces his lips down my jaw to my neck. My stomach flutters and I hug him tighter.

"Are you doing okay?" he asks.

I sigh as reality crashes back in. Do I tell him I'm utterly exhausted from pretending everything is A-OK, despite the fact that Remy's revved up the ghost stuff a thousand notches? That she scared the crap out of me at Land of Enchantment, before she trashed Dad's room, and yet I'm still compelled to smile like nothing's wrong?

I snuggle in tighter. "Yeah, I'm okay."

I hate that I can lie so easily to everyone, but I guess I've had a lot of practice over the years. I want to ask Ryan if he thinks it's easy to carry on a conversation while ignoring Remy babbling like a crazy person in the background, or how I'm supposed to keep from going insane living with this secret day after day.

I tilt my chin up and he kisses me hard. I want to lose myself in the moment, but I can't. I pull away and take a deep breath. "Do you believe in ghosts?"

My heart pounds as his smile falters.

"Um, I don't know." He shrugs. "I guess I don't *not* believe in them. Why?"

I turn my gaze to the window and see Remy rocking back and forth on her heels. "Sometimes . . . sometimes if feels like Remy is here." I hold my breath, waiting for his response.

He reaches out and takes my hand. "That's natural. I mean, she was your twin—of course you'd wish she were here, especially with what happened today."

"Yeah, but . . ." *Do it, Megan. Do it.* "Sometimes I see her. Like today in my Dad's room—she was there."

Ryan kisses my hand but doesn't say anything.

I pull my hand away and look into his eyes. "You think I'm nuts, right?"

Ryan shakes his head and reaches for my hand again. "No, of course not. I mean, I can't imagine what it was like for you; I've never lost anyone really close. But as long as you're not hearing voices, I think you're fine."

I force a smile on my face and sit up to open the bag of Chinese.

"You're *not* hearing voices, are you?"

I roll my eyes as I hand him an egg roll. "Ha! No! That *would* be nuts!"

He laughs and stuffs the egg roll in his mouth, biting it in half. "Okay," he says with his mouth full. "For movies I brought a little of everything. You pick." He spreads the DVD boxes across the table. "We have eighties: *Pretty in Pink*; romantic comedy: *Made of Honor* . . ."

I give him an incredulous look. "You asked Samantha to help pick out movies, didn't you?"

He swallows hard. "Uh. Sort of." He looks down at the DVDs, avoiding my eyes. "I thought she might know some good chick flicks."

"You do know the theme of these movies is unrequited love, don't you?"

"Oh, God." He picks up *Pretty in Pink* and looks at the back. "Oh, God." He gives me that hangdog/I'm-sorry look I see so often. "We talked after I dropped you off. Seriously, she said everything was cool. She was gonna give us some space."

I sink my face into my hands. Could this day get any worse? "Ryan, you know the girl is *head over heels* in love with you, and even if she tells you everything is cool, it's not! And what kind of a person has a 'remember we're just friends' talk and then immediately asks for help picking out movies for his girlfriend?"

His cheeks flush and he starts to stammer. "I don't, uh, know—"

"I think the word you're looking for is 'insensitive.'"

"Uh—"

"Look, Ryan, you've got to be honest, because I have enough crap going on in my life without worrying about Samantha twenty-four/seven. Do you have feelings for her?"

Ryan's mouth drops open like this is the most ridiculous thing he's ever heard. "No! She's never been anything more than a friend to me. Really!"

"Fine. Next question—and you need to be totally honest."

He furrows his brow. "Okay."

"Does a part of you get off knowing that Samantha is always waiting in the wings?"

He laces his fingers together, hangs his head, and looks sideways at me. "No!"

"It's not like it'd make you an evil person—being flattered is part of human nature. As is being jealous." I shrug. "I guess it just bugs me that you two keep having these talks about needing space, and yet this romantic evening you planned has her fingerprints on it."

"It's hard because she's right next door—it's not like I can avoid her, and she has been my friend for a long time."

"I know." I pick up *Pretty in Pink*. "And maybe I over-reacted. Molly Ringwald does end up with the hottie at the end of movie and *not* the best friend."

Ryan gives me a smoldering look. "Just like me!"

"You get brownie points for that," I say. I toss the case on the table and give him a quick kiss. "What else did you bring? And if you say season one of *Dawson's Creek*, I'm gonna punch you."

"*Dawson's Creek*?"

"It's an old TV series Nicki made me watch a gazillion times freshman year. Six seasons of unrequited love revolving around a guy in desperate need of hair intervention."

Ryan shakes his head. "No *Dawson's Creek*, but *I* picked these out: *Shaun of the Dead* and *Stardust*. I remember you said you like reading Neil Gaiman's stuff, but given my talent for screwing up . . ." He holds out *Shaun of the Dead*. "Maybe watching guys getting their brains eaten out would be more therapeutic right now."

I look around and see that Remy's nowhere in sight. "While that sounds appealing, I have a better idea." I kiss him lightly on the lips. "I don't know how long my mom will be out, but she always parks the car in the garage at night, so we'll hear her when she gets home."

I kick off my sandals, lean back on the couch, and pull Ryan down on top of me.

"Yeah, this is better than zombies," he whispers into my neck.

He kisses me and I slide my hands under his shirt. I run my fingers across his back, and I know I'll be able to shut out the madness for a while—at least until Mom comes home.

The garage door rattles up, and Ryan jumps off the couch. I pull my shirt back over my head and straighten the couch cushions. "Put a movie on. I'll get the rest of the Chinese out!"

Ryan fumbles with a DVD case, and I giggle as I take containers out of the bag and open them. "Hurry!" I say as I unwrap the chopsticks. I run into the kitchen and grab a couple of plates and then rush back into the living room.

Ryan sits back on the couch and I hand him the fried rice. He turns to me as he dumps the rice out onto our plates, and his eyes pop. "Your hair!"

I get up and look in the mirror. Total bed head, or couch head—either way, my hair screams make-out session. "I'll be right back." I go into the bathroom and pull a brush through my hair. My cheeks are flushed, but hopefully Mom will think it's from the chilies in the General Tso's chicken and not from fooling around with Ryan.

I go back into the living room and cringe. Mom is standing next to the couch with her arms folded against her chest, staring at Ryan.

"My lawyer may want to talk with you, is that okay?"

"Mom!"

Mom turns to me, her face pinched with anger. "Well, no one at the home could give me a satisfactory answer about what happened and how they can keep it from happening again, so I think I am perfectly justified getting our lawyer involved to make sure your father is getting adequate care."

I roll my eyes. "I think contacting a psychic would be more appropriate."

"And just what is that supposed to mean?" she says, giving me a look that tells me a good head-shrinking with my therapist is just a speed dial away.

Before I can answer her, Ryan stands up. "I really didn't see anything, Mrs. Sones; it seemed to happen all at once." He looks at me. "And actually, I should probably head home. We're going to a christening in Portland tomorrow, so we have to get an early start. I'll text you from the car and we can plan that hike."

"Great. I'll walk you out," I say.

Mom stares daggers at me, and Ryan shifts uncomfortably. "That's okay, Meg. I'll, uh, give you a call tomorrow." He reaches out and squeezes my hand. "Bye, Mrs. Sones."

He shuts the door and I brace myself before turning to face Mom.

"Do you want to explain yourself, young lady?"

Do I? Hell, yeah! Do I think you'll believe me? Shit, no! But I don't want the nursing home to take the rap for Remy either. Those people work crazy hours for little pay or gratitude, and I'm not gonna let Mom sic her out-for-blood lawyer on them.

"It was Remy. She was mad, and then everything just exploded."

Mom inhales deeply as her face pales. "Not this again, Megan. I won't let you do this to me again."

"I'm not doing it; Remy is. You've seen the aftermath of her temper tantrums here. Things flying off the wall, light-bulbs popping—you can't pretend that's normal. For God's sake, put two and two together!"

Mom starts to walk away, and I run after her, grabbing her arm. "How many microwaves have we replaced? How many broken picture frames have there been, or knocked over chairs? *It's all Remy.*"

Mom tries to jerk her am away but I hold tight. "Try to see her. Call her name!"

"Let go of me," she says through clenched teeth.

"Call her, damn it! Try to see her and find out why she's haunting me." I let go of her arm and look up at her face.

"*Please,* Mommy," I say, tears pouring down my cheeks. "She's still here—and maybe if you believe, you'll see her. *I need you to see her.* I need your help."

Mom's face hardens into an expressionless mask, and I look wildly around the room. "*Remy!* Mommy's looking for you! Where are you?"

"Stop it, Megan!"

"Remy! Where are you? I'll, uh, I'll make a wish! Did you hear me, Remy?" I sniff as I start walking around the room. "Star light, star bright, first star I see tonight."

Remy appears, hazy and shimmering, in front of me. "Make a wish, Meggy."

"There!" I scream, pointing to Remy. "*She's right there!*"

Mom backs away, but her eyes dart around. *Please, God, let Mom see her.* Fergus runs in and stands at her side, staring in Remy's direction. He whines, and Mom waves a hand dismissively at him.

I look at Remy and gesture toward Mom. "Remy, go to Mommy. Show her you're here!"

Mom shakes her head, but her eyes continue to search the room.

"Mom, she's right here—Remy needs you."

"No," Mom whispers. Her lower lip trembles. "Stop it, Megan."

I look back and forth between Remy and Mom—neither

one seeing the other—and fall to my knees. "You're her mother, why can't you see her?" I point up at Remy again. *"She's right there!"*

Tears well up in Mom's eyes, and her face crumples. "Why are you doing this to me?"

"I need you to see her," I say, sobbing. "I can't do this by myself anymore."

"What you need is help." She shakes her head and turns away from me to go into the kitchen.

"Don't bother calling Dr. Macardo! I'm not crazy and you can't make me go." I curl up on the floor and Fergus lies down next to me. I wrap my arms around him and cry as Remy skips in a circle around us.

∽ FIVE ∽

A car blows past me and I wobble on my bike. I grip the handlebars tighter and keep my legs pumping in a steady rhythm. I hope Luke is home. It's only seven thirty, so I'm thinking it's too early for him to be heading to Land of Enchantment. Of course, he's probably asleep and won't be too excited about my waking him up, but I'm desperate.

I see the sign welcoming tourists to the North Conway outlet strip, and just past it is Luke's purple house.

I pedal harder and then brake by the front walkway. Lawn ornaments line the path and I can imagine what Nicki would say if she were here. "This array of gnomes, plastic ducks, and spotted fawns is clearly a sign of mental illness, and you'd be crazy to go in that house."

I sigh. Seeing as 'crazy' is my new middle name, what do I have to lose?

As I roll my bike toward the house, I try to shake off the feeling that I'm sneaking around on Ryan. I know I'm not doing anything wrong, I'm just here about Remy, and the fluttering in my stomach is all about nerves and not about keeping something from my boyfriend. And I *tried* to tell Ryan about her, I needed him to know, but it was pretty obvious that pushing the whole ghost thing would've sent him running—like Mom.

I lean my bike against the front porch. Wind chimes tinkle as the cool morning breeze blows past, carrying the scent of lilacs. I walk slowly up the creaking steps and my stomach flips nervously. What if Luke can't help me? What if I'm stuck with Remy for the rest of my life?

I ring the bell and hear feet shuffling inside. The door opens and a small, round woman in a floral housecoat looks up at me. She fingers a long, thick braid of white hair draped over her shoulder and clucks her tongue.

"Oh," she says as she reaches a hand toward my arm. "You poor thing, come inside and let Nona help you."

The moment her fingers touch my skin, the nervous feeling disappears.

She leads me into a room just off the front entryway and points to an overstuffed chair.

"Sit," she says gently.

I drop down into the chair and she looks me up and down. "You're too young to have such a dark cloud surrounding you."

"I'm—I'm here to see Luke," I say, unable to look away from her piercing blue eyes.

"Shh." Nona reaches out and places her hands on my temples. "So much pain," she whispers.

A sense of calm seems to radiate from her fingers and fills my body. I sink back into the chair and breathe deeply.

"That's it," she says.

"Nona!"

I bolt up in the chair. Luke is standing in the doorway with his hands on his hips.

Nona scoffs. "Don't start with me, Luka. At seventy-nine I tell you what to do and not vice versa!"

Luke rushes to her side just in time to catch Nona as she wobbles on her feet. "At seventy-nine I'd think you'd know better," he says as he leads her to another chair.

Nona fans her face for a few seconds and then points to me. "If you saw what I did, you'd know this can't wait!"

Luke looks at me, his brow furrowed. "Megan, what are you doing here?"

"I thought maybe you could help me with—"

Luke shakes his head and mouths the word "no."

"You never mind him; I can help you and the little girl," Nona says.

She looks to the window, and I turn and see Remy standing quietly, the curtains floating gently through her.

"You see her too?" I ask.

"Is there something here, Nona?" Luke asks. He peers around the room, but his eyes don't stop on Remy. I give him a quizzical look. He puts a finger up to his lip and shakes his head. It's obvious he doesn't want me to talk about what happened at Land of Enchantment, but I don't know why.

"Yes, there is a little girl who needs my help."

"Nona, enough already. You almost fainted."

Nona shakes her head and pushes herself up from her chair. "*I* can handle this, Luka. Make yourself useful and bring over the chair. I'll sit if that'll get you off an old woman's back."

Luke drags the chair over across from mine. Nona plops down and reaches out for my hand.

"It's hard work healing with these old hands of mine, but God gave me this gift," she says, glaring at Luke, "and I won't turn anyone away—not when I can make them better."

I look at Luke biting his lip as he stands behind Nona's chair.

"Tell me what happened to your sister," Nona says quietly. "I must know everything so I can help her move on."

I take a deep breath. How did she know Remy was my sister? My next thought is that I don't want to even think about the accident, let alone give a blow by blow. I shake my head, trying to keep the tears at bay.

"It's okay," Nona whispers. "Let it go." She gently takes both of my hands, and I feel that sense of calm coursing through me again. "Tell Nona."

I close my eyes and see Remy and me sitting in the backseat of our old orange Volvo. "We . . . we were driving to a restaurant for my dad's birthday. Mom was going to meet us there."

Dad was going too fast along the river. We were running late, because Remy had to find her favorite purple sundress. It was too short, and Mom was forever putting it in the bag of clothes to bring to Goodwill, and Remy was forever fishing it out.

Remy dumped several bags piled in the sun porch out onto the floor, making a total mess, until she found it. Dad didn't even make her pick up all the clothes, and I knew Mom would have a fit when we all got home.

My lip trembles as I remember I'd been looking forward to Remy getting in trouble when Mom saw she was wearing the dress.

"Keep going," Nona whispers.

I nod and continue. "The sky got really, really dark.

Lightning streaked past and Remy, my sister, counted the seconds until the thunder clapped. 'It's close, Daddy,' she said, and then the rain came.

"I could barely see out the windshield, and then there was another flash of lightning ahead of us. Just as the thunder boomed, rocks rained down onto the car as the cliff on the side of the road gave way." I swallow hard. "The landslide pushed us off the road and the car flipped twice before we hit the river.

"The car landed on its side and was swept downstream until it slammed up against a boulder. Remy's window smashed, and then water came in."

I close my eyes and hear the sound of the river in my head—our screams. "Remy tried to undo her seat belt as the water filled the car. I was hanging from my booster seat, and I tried to reach her but I couldn't. I cried for Dad to help, but he was unconscious in the front seat and just about under too. By the time the current pushed the car upright again, Remy wasn't breathing and my dad never woke up."

Nona squeezes my hand as she rocks back and forth. I feel surprisingly light and calm despite the fact that I just relived the accident.

She drops my hands and leans back in her chair. "Your sister is searching for something," Nona says. "She won't leave until she finds it. I'm picking up helplessness from her—and fear. Great fear."

Nona pulls some tissues out from her cleavage under the housecoat and mops her face. "Luka, I need to lie down and rest before my afternoon appointments. Can you help me?"

Luke nods and helps Nona stand. "I can't lead your sister to the light; she won't see it until she finds what she's looking for. You come back again, and I will see if I can talk with her when I'm feeling stronger."

"Don't go," Luke says softly to me, and then he leads Nona out of the room.

"What are you looking for, Remy?" I whisper, watching her rocking back and forth on her heels.

"Hey, let's go outside where we can talk," Luke says when he returns. I follow him out through the back of the house to a gazebo surrounded by tall grass and wildflowers.

"How are you feeling?" he asks as we take a seat on the cushioned bench.

"I don't know why, but I actually feel better than I have in a long time. I thought talking about the accident would make me feel worse, but . . ."

Luke nods. "Among other things, Nona's an empath— she takes away people's pain. It's not permanent or anything, and it really knocks it out of her, but you should be feeling pretty good for a while."

"Oh, great, so I pretty much beat up your grandmother?"

A half smile creeps across his face and he runs his fingers through his hair. "Pretty much, but she asked for it."

My shoulders slump. "I am so sorry. I never would have let her do that if I knew. I just came here to see you. I was hoping you could help me with Remy."

He looks up toward his house, and then back at me. "About that. I want to help you, but I have to be careful because Nona doesn't actually know I inherited the spooky gene. As far as she's concerned, I'm as psychic as the ceramic kittens hanging on the side of the house over there."

I stare at him incredulously. "But how can she not know? From what I just experienced, I'd be surprised you could hide anything from her."

Luke looks at the house again and shrugs. "I guess I'm a pretty good actor. There've been a few close calls—it's not easy pretending not to notice nasty stuff racing around a room."

I give him a look. "Tell me about it."

Luke smiles. "Yeah, I guess you know what I'm talking about."

"But I don't understand. I *have* to pretend Remy doesn't exist so I don't get put under heavy sedation and carted off to the loony bin." I shake my head. Given what happened last night, I should probably be on alert for ambulance drivers lurking in the bushes, waiting to ambush me. "But all this ghost stuff is just part of your DNA—why hide it?"

Luke laughs. "Because I don't want to spend my life listening to people who want to know if their dearly departed think they should cut the spoiled grandkids out of their will, or if they really meant to leave all of their money to the dog."

I look at him with wide eyes. "Seriously?"

"Sadly, yes. There's this one woman who comes in just about every other week to talk to her dead mother about whether or not she should change her hair color or break up with the guy she's dating. And some man came in two days ago with his Siamese cat, Mr. Bootsie, to see if Nona could ask it if his wife is cheating on him."

"Was she cheating?"

Luke shakes his head. "We have many talents, but communicating with pampered pets is not one of them." He shrugs. "I grew up watching a parade of people come to my house needing spiritual guidance for the most mundane things, and I knew I didn't want to go there. I pretended not to see the ghosts, and Nona directed all of her attention on training my sister." Luke bows his head.

"Ari told me about Kayla," I say quietly. Luke doesn't say

anything, and that calm feeling I had starts to ebb. I purse my lips and wonder if Luke is grouping me with all the other nuts who come here for help. "You know, I should go. I didn't want to bother you, I just . . ."

I start to rise and he puts a hand on my arm, sending an electric shock through me. "Don't go. I didn't mean to make you feel like I didn't want you here. I'm actually *really* glad you came."

"You can read minds too?"

He gently tugs on my arm and I sit down again. "Not exactly, but with someone like you, I can get a general sense of how they're feeling."

"Someone like me?"

"Someone who sees ghosts. People who are closed to that plane of existence are really hard to read, but you're pretty transparent—no pun intended—and when I met you in the costume room, it wasn't hard to pick up on the fact that you were terrified."

I picture the girl lying on the forest floor and nod. "When Remy came to me in that room she showed me something—something really horrible. And ever since, she's been popping up more and more, and freaking out, and I don't know why or what to do."

He takes my hand, and a warm, prickling sensation runs through me. I think of Ryan and feel guilty for a second until I remind myself that this is just business to Luke. I let the feeling of calm radiate from his hand and know he's doing what Nona did—taking away my pain. I know it isn't fair to dump this on him, but it feels so good to be free from the pain for a while.

"What did she show you?" he whispers. "Picture it so I can see it too—take in all of the details."

He takes my other hand and leans in closer to me, making me catch my breath for a second. I feel connected and close to him. I close my eyes. I see the girl and force myself to really look at her. Her outfit is different from anything that was on the rack in the costume room. The blouse, soaked in blood, is very detailed with eyelet trim and embroidered flowers across the top edge, instead of the garish red satin trim on the costumes.

Part of the blouse is unlaced and pulled aside to expose the jagged hole in her chest. I quickly move up to her face and gasp for a second, thinking it's me, but it's just a girl with dark hair like mine. The pale skin on her cheeks is spattered with blood, and her lips are parted—with more blood trickling down from one corner. Her blue eyes stare blankly up at the sky. I look away from her face and see the leaves and dirt of the forest floor marked with crimson.

I shake my head to erase the image and push up from the bench to stand at the rail of the gazebo. Tears sting my eyes as I look out on the gardens, trying to fill my mind with images of flowers instead of the dead girl's stare. "*Why* would Remy show me *that*?"

The bench creaks, and Luke stands next to me, exhaling loudly. "Wow. That was the last thing I was expecting. I've seen some pretty weird stuff before, but . . ."

"I probably should've warned you."

"Yeah, a little heads-up might've been nice. I gotta say, I'm surprised how well you're keeping it together. I would've figured something like that might have you a little more freaked out."

My eyes follow a butterfly flitting around in front of us, and I shrug. "Telling myself everything's A-OK—no matter how freaky it gets—has been my mantra since Remy came back just after the accident. She was lying in her bed right next to mine, singing.

"For a second I thought the crash was just a dream and Remy was still alive and my dad wasn't in the hospital. I was so happy, I called out for my parents. Only, my mom came in *alone*. She turned on my lights, and that's when I found out I could see *through* Remy—and my mom couldn't see her at all. My mom kept telling me I was dreaming and to wake up, but I still remember she looked at me like I was crazy when I insisted Remy was in her bed.

"After that, plus some forced therapy, I got used to

pretending Remy wasn't there, but it's getting harder to do now. In the past, she'd only appear every few months, and most of the time she didn't say anything, but now she's in haunting overdrive."

Tears sting my eyes. "I'm getting scared, and I don't want to do this alone anymore—that's why I came here today. I mean, when I found out you could see her and talk to her, it was *such* a relief, because in the back of my mind I always wondered if maybe I was crazy."

Luke reaches out and brushes a tear from my cheek. "Hey, it's okay. I'll help you figure this out. And do you want to know something?"

I sniff. "What?"

"It was a big relief knowing *you* could see Remy too. I haven't been able to talk to anyone about this stuff since Kayla died."

"*Died?* I thought she was just missing. Ari didn't say she . . . you know . . ."

Luke walks back over to the bench and sits. He leans back and turns his gaze to the gardens, looking lost and sad.

"Ari doesn't know. The cops don't know. But the night she disappeared I felt like she was in the house with me. I felt her wanting me to take care of Ari for her. And then there was nothing—she was gone. I've tried calling her back, but Kayla knows enough about ghosts to not want to stick around. She moved on—she's at peace."

I walk over and sit down next him on the bench and reach out for his hand. "I'm sorry."

He leans into me. My heart skips a beat as our shoulders touch, and I can't help thinking I shouldn't be holding his hand and sitting this close to him. But I don't want to stop either.

"I just wish I knew *what* happened to her."

"Yeah," I whisper. "I'm a little surprised she'd come back and be worried about Ari, though. I know her home life isn't perfect, but she seems pretty strong."

Luke pulls away from me and stretches his long legs out in front of him. "Ari's complicated. She's got a lot to give, but she needs more in return. I think it's because her mother passed away when she was little and her dad married Patty. As you said, things are not exactly stable at that house—probably worse than you can imagine—but I owe them big-time.

"After Ari met Kayla on the playground when they were little, the Roys took us under their wings, so to speak. They've helped us out a lot over the years. Paid for our tuition at school—even painting lessons when I was younger. So when things are rough at home, I try to keep Ari on an even keel to pay them back—for Kayla."

Luke to the rescue, I almost say out loud. As much as he doesn't want to admit it, he obviously inherited Nona's desire to help people. I wonder if Luke realizes Ari is in love with him. It's not hard imagining why.

As soon as the words form in my head, I push them out. I am not like Samantha; I don't steal boyfriends—or Ari's potential boyfriend. And I need to remember that the feeling I get from Luke is just part of a job, whether or not he gets paid for it like Nona.

Luke clears his throat. "But back to that girl—it looked like her heart . . ."

"Was missing. I thought maybe she was in one of the costumes from Land of Enchantment, but don't you think her clothes look old-fashioned, like maybe it happened a *really* long time ago?"

"Yeah, they don't make clothes like that anymore."

I nod. "Thank God for that. Well, not that she had her chest carved open, but seeing as I just signed on to play Snow White, it's a relief to know that this was something that happened in the past and not one of Remy's scary-things-to-come visions."

"Ghosts can travel the time streams—they have access to all kinds of things in the past, present, and future, but I don't know why Remy chose *that* particular scene to show you, except the girl kind of looked like you."

"Yeah, I noticed that, only her eyes were blue and mine are—"

"Brown."

"Yeah," I say, liking that he noticed what color my eyes are. I picture Nicki smirking at me and saying, "Did someone forget they have a boyfriend?" again.

No, I tell myself, but there's something really nice about being able to talk openly about my sister—something I can't do with Nicki or Ryan.

I turn to Luke and inch closer to him. "So what about Remy? Is there anything you can do?"

"Nona said Remy was looking for something, and that she was scared. So the first thing to do is figure out why. Was there something she always carried with her—a doll or even a blanket?"

"Can't you just ask her?"

Luke gives me a weary smile. "I don't know, that vision kind of knocked me on my ass." He gives me a wink and a crooked smile. "I guess I'm no better than Nona. I asked for it. But I've never actually tried to talk to a ghost—they usually come to me first."

I smile back at him and try to ignore the way he makes my stomach flutter. *Ryan,* I scream in my head.

"So could Remy be looking for a toy or something?" he asks.

"No, she actually made fun of me because I had a stuffed bear that I took everywhere—until it got left in the car after the accident. I don't know what happened to him." I sigh, knowing this isn't the time to lament the loss of Mr. B-bear. "There was this dress she liked, but . . ." Tears well up in my eyes again. "But she was buried in it.

"Could she be looking for my mom? I told my mom Remy was in the house last night. I told Remy to go to her, hoping my mom would finally see her."

"And?"

"And nothing, other than my mom thinks I'm some kind of sociopath who gets off causing her mental anguish. I just don't understand why I can see Remy and she can't. And it's weird, because Remy doesn't seem to see her either—or my dad. She was even asking where my dad was and . . ."

My eyes grow wide. "Oh my God! She was asking me where our dad was yesterday. She was right in the room with him, but it was like she didn't know. He never woke up after the accident—he's on life support. Could she be looking for him? Waiting for him before she can, you know, move on?"

Luke nods, looking excited. "That might be it. He might be in some sort of limbo and she needs to connect with him before she can move on."

I purse my lips as tears pool in my eyes. "My dad was her favorite—she and my mom were always butting heads."

I look at Luke. "That's it. I know it. She's been waiting for him all this time."

"It makes sense; that could be what's keeping her here."

I jump up, wiping my eyes. "I've got to talk to my mom."

"Wait! What're you going to do? You can't just ask your mother to . . . you know . . ."

"I have to. It's time Remy and my father found some peace."

⌒ SIX ⌒

efore you ask, I don't want to talk about it," I say as I get into Nicki's car. "But thanks for picking me up."

Nicki raises one eyebrow. "Come on, you have to tell me. She hasn't sent you to Dr. Macardo in years."

"It's none of your business," I snap, and immediately I feel guilty. "I'm sorry. Maybe I should just walk home." I put my hand on the door, and Nicki pulls on my arm. I let go and slump down in the seat.

"Come on, Megan, what's going on?"

I shake my head and look away, staring at the North Conway Mental Health Clinic sign. How do I tell Nicki I want to pull the plug on my own father?

Dr. Macardo did agree that thinking about pulling the plug was normal. Telling my mother Remy was in the room was apparently another matter entirely, though. Of course, I'd like Dr. Macardo to spend some time at my house observing my mother, and then see who should get the passive-aggressive label he tossed around numerous times during our session.

A half smile curls my lips. At least he convinced Mom to make a session for herself. I wonder if Dr. Macardo will have Mom draw some family pictures with his stupid box of broken crayons. Maybe then Mom would finally come to grips with the fact that she shut down and left me after the accident, and that she's not the only one who misses Dad and Remy.

"Okay," I say finally. I let out a long sigh and brace myself for Nicki's reaction. "I asked my mother what she thought about taking my dad off the machines." I pause, hating what comes next. "And she thought I needed to talk to Dr. Macardo about why I wanted to *murder* my own father."

Nicki gasps, and I'm glad I left out the part about Remy. "Would-be killer" sounds so much better than "crazy psychopath who also sees ghosts."

"Yeah, I know. I'm a monster—Charles Manson Jr."

"God, Megan. No." I turn to her and she opens her arms and I let her hug me. "I've . . . I've thought about that too, you know—the machines. Especially after the last time I went with you to the nursing home. I just didn't want to say anything because we've never really talked about *that*, and I didn't know how you felt."

I still don't know exactly how I feel about it. After being with Luke I was so sure it was the right thing to do for Dad *and* Remy. But after seeing the horror on Mom's face, I started second-guessing myself. Is it really murder?

But it seemed like Dr. Macardo totally understood. I did my homework and I know the statistics. The chance of recovery after six months in a vegetative state is slim to none. The rare instances get a lot of press, but with six months being the standard cutoff, where does that leave Dad after ten years?

Maybe getting my head shrunk today wasn't such a bad idea after all. If anything, Dr. Marcado's not judging me harshly made me feel slightly less monsterish.

Nicki holds me tight and the tears come again. "He's never getting better—the doctors keep telling her that. All of the tests prove there's no brain activity, but his eyes fluttered open that *one* time right after the crash, and she thinks he could wake up still."

I pull away and look out at the office sign. "And maybe she's right, it happens, but when I saw my dad yesterday, I just knew he's not there anymore. I just knew he's not going to wake up, and now she hates me more than ever."

"Hey," Nicki says. "Your mom doesn't hate you—"

"Oh, yes, she does! Maybe she didn't hate me before, maybe it was more indifference, but you should see the way she looks at me now. She *hates* me."

"She's scared. It's a huge, hard decision to make, and—"

"And she said she's not gonna do it. Ever. He's going to keep hanging on, wasting away more and more." Leaving Remy alone.

"Give her some time to think about it—cool off. It's not like it's an easy decision to make."

"So what does that say about me?"

She squeezes my hand. "That you know this isn't what your dad would've wanted. Would you want to live like that?"

I shake my head.

"Look, why don't you spend the night at my house tonight? That'll give both of you a break."

I sniff and look away from her. "Um, actually, Ari called and asked if I wanted to hang out."

Nicki starts the car. "Oh, why didn't you have *Ari* pick you up then?"

"Because you already said you would!"

"I thought you might need someone to talk to, but you

and Ari can have a nice chat about all of this." Nicki puts the car in reverse, and then pulls out of the parking space a little too fast.

"Nicki, it's not like that, and I don't want to talk to Ari about this stuff. She just sounded lonely. I didn't want to hurt her feelings. And when I told her you were picking me up, she said she'd *love* for you to come too. I only said yes because I thought you'd be with me."

Nicki gives me an incredulous look. "I don't for one second believe Ari wants me to come over. You should've seen her staring daggers at me at the tryouts when the new director clapped after my audition."

"Seriously, she told me to ask you over. I was talking to her when you pulled up. She said her pool is open—and heated. And get this, she told me to tell you they have a movie-viewing room and a bunch of bootlegged recordings of Broadway shows—shows that were never supposed to be filmed."

Nicki turns to me quickly with one eyebrow raised again. "Like what?"

"I didn't ask—that's more your deal—but she *obviously* only mentioned it because she wanted you to come. And Luke said Ari is kind of complicated, so she—"

"*Oh,*" Nicki says, drawing out the word. "And when were you talking to *Luke?*"

My cheeks burn. "I . . . just . . . kind of ran into him—an out-of-the-blue kind of thing."

Nicki rolls her eyes. "Uh-huh. Good thing you and Ryan will be working closely this summer."

"I'll have you know Ryan and I have our summer completely planned. When we're not at Land of Enchantment, we're going to be hiking the Presidential Range. Well, we've started with some of the smaller mountains to work up to the big guns, but we have a book where we can check off each hike, and I started a scrapbook with pictures of us at the summits."

Nicki yawns. "Scrapbook? Must be love. Anyway, someone on this Broadway message board said there's a bootlegged copy of *Dirty Rotten Scoundrels* making the rounds. I wonder if Ari has that. I'd love to see Norbert Leo Butz."

"Norbert Leo *Butz*?"

"Don't let the name fool you, the man is a comedic genius—a genius with a voice to die for." Nicki glances down at the center console, grabs her CD carrier, and tosses it over to me. "See if you can find the soundtrack—it's hilarious."

"I take it this means you've changed your mind about going to Ari's?"

She smiles at me. "Sure, let's get our suits and head over. I'm not sure I'll go swimming, though."

"It'll be just us girls," I say, knowing Nicki feels over-exposed in a bathing suit.

"We'll see."

Nicki and I stand on Ari's front steps, staring at the door knocker—a tarnished brass rabbit with an arrow through its chest. My hand is poised over the knocker part, which is shaped in the form of a bow with the string pulled back in a wide arc.

"I can't do it," I say, pulling my hand back.

"Yeah, that's more than a little disturbing," Nicki whispers.

"Let's just ring the bell again." I push the button, and the seemingly endless chimes begin again. "Someone's *got* to hear that."

Nicki cocks her head and examines the rabbit. "Where would a person even find a knocker like that? Creep and Barrel?" She grimaces and pushes the bell again.

"I'm coming!" a voice yells from inside.

"That sounds like Ari's stepmother," I say in a hushed voice. "Brace yourself."

The door flies open and Miss Patty gawks at us. I force myself to keep my smile steady as I take Patty in. She's for-gotten to draw on one of her eyebrows, and her mascara is smudged and gathered in the creases under her eyes. She's wearing a pink velour jumpsuit that's a little too snug across her stomach, and several of her hair extensions are dangling by their clips.

"Morgan!" she croaks. She wobbles a bit, and then steadies herself by grabbing the doorframe. She squints and leans toward me, alcohol burning on her breath. "No, it's Megan," she says, giving me a wink. "I never forget an enchanted team member."

"I'll bet," I say, trying not to stare at her one eyebrow.

I guess she has the right to do whatever she wants after business hours, but hearing her slur her words and watching her clutch the doorframe in order to hold herself up is a stark contrast to the overly bubbly woman I interviewed with. "Ari invited us over. This is Nicki—she's not an enchanted team member."

Miss Patty stumbles back a few steps and opens her arms wide. "Well, let me welcome you to our humble abode."

We step in and it's obvious there's nothing humble about this place. Marble staircase, crystal chandeliers—it's like walking into Cinderella's palace at Land of Enchantment, but all of this stuff looks real.

"Deborah!" Miss Patty screeches. Nicki and I jump and exchange looks. "Deborah!"

A small woman with gray hair done up in a tight knot and wearing a maid's uniform hurries down the hallway toward us. "Yes, Miss?"

"Where's Ari?"

"Last I saw her she was up in the study."

Miss Patty jerks her head toward us. "Oh, well, Ari's always got her nose in a book." She chews on her lip, nibbling off what's left of her hot pink lipstick, and then turns back to Deborah. "Why don't you show these girls to the entertainment room? I'd better find Ari myself."

"Certainly, Miss." Deborah gives us a weary smile. "Right this way, ladies." She leads us down the long hall and into a large room with dark wood-paneled walls. "Make yourselves comfortable and I'll get you some iced tea."

"Thanks," I say, thinking it would suck to be a maid here with people barking orders.

After Deborah leaves, Nicki twirls a finger at the side of her head. "Ari's stepmom is craaazy!" she says. "And apparently cocktail hour comes way earlier here than at my house."

I nod. "Told you things weren't all 'happily ever after' at Casa Roy."

"And look at this room," she says.

I walk in a circle, taking it in. Leather couches, ginormous flat-screen TV, shelves lined with DVDs and old VHS tapes, tapestries depicting various hunting scenes, and a multitude of taxidermic animal heads staring around the room with blank glass eyes. "Decorating with dead things— very classy."

Nicki walks up to three bear heads mounted in a row on the wall, their mouths frozen in never-ending snarls. "So this is what happened to the Three Bears. Wouldn't Martha Stewart have a seizure if she saw these hanging on the wall?"

"Some dead relative killed them in Germany—Black Forest. Hunting was big back then for the aristocracy."

I jump and turn around. Ari is standing in the doorway with her arms folded across her chest, eyes narrowed, staring coldly at me. "Glad you could make it, *Nicki*," she says, her eyes still focused on me.

My face flushes as Ari's eyes continue to bore into me with such intense scrutiny that I immediately regret feeling sorry for her and agreeing to come over. "Uh, hey, Ari," I say softly, wishing she'd stop looking at me like that.

She saunters into the room, running her fingers along the edge of a leather couch laden with animal pelts. She stops a few feet away from me and plops down in an overstuffed chair. "So, *Megan*, what's up?" Her lips turn up ever so slightly to make a tight smile.

"Um, up?" I stammer. "Nothing's up, we just came over to see you—you know, you called and, uh . . ." I give Nicki a sideways look and see she's just as puzzled by Ari's ice-queen act as I am.

"Hey, did you look over all of our music yet?" Nicki asks, coming to my rescue. "At first I was worried all the focus on old jazz might not pull in the tourist crowds, but after I've listened to the songs a few times, I'm excited. You know I love Broadway, but this will be a nice change."

"Yeah, and lucky you getting to sing 'Someone to Watch Over Me' all by yourself."

"Actually, that one *was* from a Broadway play, but—"

"So, *Megan*," Ari says, interrupting Nicki. "Did you do anything interesting today? Or see anyone interesting?"

My mind scrambles. Would Dr. Macardo qualify as interesting?

And then it clicks. Luke.

Somehow Ari knows I saw Luke and she's beyond pissed off thinking I was pulling a *Samantha Lee Darling* on her. My heart races as I struggle to come up with some sort of reason for being there—a reason that doesn't involve Remy.

"Oh, well, uh," I stammer. I swallow hard and then it comes to me. I sit on a couch opposite her and try to look self-conscious. "This is sort of embarrassing, but you'll love this—you too, Nicki. Remember how you told me about Luke's grandmother, you know, about her being a so-called psychic?"

Nicki sits on another couch, giving me a where-is-this-going look.

"Yeah," Ari deadpans.

"Well, I got this crazy idea that maybe she might be

able to like, um, look in to my future and tell me something about Ryan."

"Ryan?" Ari asks, surprise in her eyes.

I swallow again. "Yeah, like if we were destined to be together." I give a pained smile. "Pathetic, huh?"

Nicki bursts out laughing. "Oh my God! I *knew* you were going to go there sometime. It was freshman year when you asked me about that place."

Ari's face softens. "Freshman year?"

Nicki snorts. "Yeah, she wanted to go—what was it for—something about Jason? Oh, man, I *cannot* believe you actually went!" She sits up straight and folds her hands in her lap. "So how many kids are you and Ryan going to have? Boys or girls? Was she able to tell you about your future pets too?"

I roll my eyes. "Ha, ha. I didn't even get a reading or anything—Mrs. Amador wasn't feeling well. I did see Luke for a few minutes, though. Did he tell you, Ari?"

Ari sits up straight too. "No. But I was driving by . . . uh, on my way to get my nails done and saw you at his house."

"Oh, well, I'm sure he'll tell you all about pathetic me hoping to get my cards read."

Deborah comes in carrying a silver tray with a pitcher of iced tea and glasses. I could kiss her for her perfect timing. She pours us each a glass and I gulp mine down hoping the cool liquid might do something to get rid of the burning sensation in my cheeks.

"Anything else, Miss?" Deborah asks.

Ari waves a hand dismissively. "No, we're good."

When Deborah leaves I chance looking at Ari again, and I'm relieved to see Happy Ari has returned. "So," she says, "how many kids would you want with Ryan?"

"Um, I never really thought that far into the future," I say.

Ari nods. "Yeah, can't say I blame you."

"Huh?" Nicki asks, looking back and forth between Ari and me.

"Samantha Lee Darling," Ari and I say in unison and burst into giggles.

"Oh, don't encourage her paranoia about Samantha, it's beyond demeaning. She should trust Ryan or dump his ass!"

"Well, not all of us are as perfect as you," Ari says. She jumps up before Nicki can respond and walks over to a large wooden hutch. She opens the doors and pulls out a bottle of vodka and gives it a shake. "Who wants to spice up their iced tea?"

I look at Nicki, who scowls and shakes her head ever so slightly. She doesn't drink because she says alcohol is bad for her voice. Since Nicki doesn't imbibe, I don't either, especially after a very unfortunate experience at the reception for my aunt Kerry's third wedding when I was fourteen. Everyone there was totally boozing it up because the groom, a truck driver with a huge beer belly and rundown double-wide, was an even bigger loser than husbands one and two.

I snuck way too many margaritas and ended up puking for hours in the hotel room. Luckily, I was sharing the room with my cousin Nora, who was just slightly less inebriated, and I blamed my upset stomach the next day on the pork rind appetizers at the reception.

Ari cocks her head at us. "Don't tell me you two don't drink."

Nicki folds her arms across her chest. "You shouldn't either—it'll ruin your voice."

"Seeing as *you* get all the solos, I don't have to worry about that. How about you, Megan? You said you can't sing for shit."

"I guess I'll try a little," I say, avoiding looking at Nicki. Just because she can't drink doesn't really mean I have to go along, and it's not like I'm looking to repeat margarita madness.

Ari walks over and refills my glass with vodka and iced tea. She holds hers up and I raise mine. "To a truly *enchanted* summer," she says as we clink glasses.

Nicki ignores the toast and places her glass on the table. "Megan said you've got some shows we could watch."

Ari takes a long drink and then smiles at Nicki. "I'm kind of in the mood for something *dark*. Do you like *Sweeney Todd*?"

I grimace. Nicki had nightmares for weeks after watching the movie version of *Sweeney Todd*, and seeing people get their throats slit and ground up into meat pies wasn't something I was dying to see again either.

Nicki pales and shakes her head. "Anything a little more upbeat than cannibalistic barbers?"

Ari laughs and gets up. "Come over here and you can see what we've got."

I watch them walk over to a shelf stuffed with DVDs and videotapes and take another sip of my drink, the too-strong vodka burning its way down my throat. Ari certainly hasn't mastered the fine art of bartending.

"Meggy," a voice whispers right next to my ear.

I jerk my head and choke on the iced tea. Remy is standing next to me wringing the hem of her dress in her hands. "Come quick!" She skips toward the door and I'm hoping she'll just keep going and disappear, but she turns back and beckons to me. "Hurry, Meggy!"

I sigh. *Please, God, no pyrotechnics tonight.*

⤳ SEVEN ⤳

After excusing myself to the bathroom, I follow Remy down the hall and groan as she races up the stairs.

"Remy!" I hiss. "We can't go up there!" She fades away and I bite my lower lip and consider turning around and heading back to Nicki and Ari.

She reappears at the top and leans over the banister. "Hurry, Meggy, it's bad!"

My stomach lurches and I brace myself for another Remy meltdown. What could she possibly be so freaked out about? I look around for the maid or Miss Patty, and then hike my purse strap over my shoulder and tiptoe up the stairs. I wince every time the polished steps creak under my feet. "Remy, we really shouldn't be doing this."

I reach the landing and see Remy walk into a room about halfway down the hall. As I get closer I hear Miss Patty's voice. "What the *hell* did you show her?"

My heart races and I want to turn around, but Remy's calling me, her voice starting to take on that frantic tone she uses before everything goes to hell.

"I don't give a crap what you promised her," Patty continues. "I'm her mother and I want to see what you showed her so I can do some damage control before she goes and gets another bee in her bonnet and someone gets hurt."

A deep, dark laugh answers Patty, sending chills up my spine. A man's voice—too low to be Mr. Roy's—says something, but I can't make it out.

"Well, I'm the only mother she knows, thanks to you!"

"Meggy," Remy's voice implores from the room.

I take a step toward the doorway, peek inside, and catch my breath. Miss Patty is standing in front of a large gilded mirror, identical to the one in her office, but her reflection isn't showing. Instead, a man's long, narrow face, its edges blurred and smoky, floats in the center of the glass.

"Yes," the face says, drawing out the word mockingly. "The only mother she's ever known—and one she holds in utmost contempt. You know what she thinks of you, you ask me all the time, so why are you so concerned about her all of a sudden?"

Miss Patty puts her drink to her lips and drains it. The ice rattles in the empty glass as she holds it tightly at her side. "She's got that look again."

"It hasn't bothered you in the past."

"Well, it bothers me now!" Patty snaps. "We have everything we need, but it's never enough for her—she wants more and more and he always gives it to her. It isn't right."

The face smirks. Two hands with incredibly long fingers and dark pointed nails appear in front of the face's chin and clap slowly a couple of times. "Oh, he does love to spoil her, doesn't he? How do you feel knowing her every whim will be satisfied, yet he denied you your heart's greatest desire?"

"He would've done it if he hadn't consulted Ari first! Like it was any of her damn business if we wanted more kids."

"Or it could be that he didn't want to have a child with you for other reasons. You're hardly royalty. Where was it he found you again?" The fingers of one hand tap the chin once. "Oh, yes, in a stripper bar."

"Shut up!" Patty shrieks and she throws her drink at the mirror's surface.

I want to leave, but I'm rooted to the spot. I want the mirror to shatter and that face to stop talking, but the glass bounces off the mirror and breaks as it hits the floor. Ice cubes skitter across the stone tiles along with the broken shards of the cocktail glass. Miss Patty stands frozen, staring at her own reflection, which now fills the mirror. I see her eye makeup drawn down her cheeks by her tears.

Remy appears at my side, her eyes wide with fear. "Run, Meggy!"

My phone rings and I gasp. I bolt down the hall as Miss Patty calls out, "Ari? Ari, is that you?"

I race down the stairs as I fumble through my purse for my phone and turn the sound off. I pass the bathroom, and then double back, go in, and shut the door. I hear Miss Patty thunder down the stairs. "What's the matter, Ari? Couldn't wait to have your little friend spy on me, so you had to do it yourself?"

Miss Patty stops in front of the bathroom. "Ari," she says, her voice dripping with venom. "Come out, we need to talk."

Oh great, she thinks I'm Ari. "Um, it's me, Megan," I call out with a shaky voice. "I'm . . . I'm just finishing up in the bathroom." I flush the toilet, hoping she'll think I was in here all along.

"Oh! I . . . I forgot you were here. I . . . just, well, I'll go get Ari. Sorry," Miss Patty says through the door.

I listen to her footsteps leading away and take in a deep breath. What the *hell* just happened, and what the *hell* was in that mirror? I quickly look up at the bathroom mirror and I'm relieved to see my own face—pale and drawn as it is—instead of the horrible one that was talking to Patty.

Why are you doing this to me, Remy?

I shake my head. Why does Remy do any of the things she does? "If only Dad could be with you," I whisper. "Then you could rest and I could get on with my life without seeing girls with their chest carved open or floating heads in mirrors!"

I grip the counter and take a deep breath. Getting carted off to the loony bin is actually sounding somewhat appealing—as long as Remy can't come, that is.

I look at the missed call and see it was Ryan. Why did he have to go to Portland today? We could've done something and I wouldn't be here, hiding in the bathroom!

Well, I can't stay in here forever. I just hope Miss Patty isn't lurking around, ready to ask why I was spying on her.

I open the door and see Patty having a heated discussion with Ari outside the entertainment room. They both turn my way as I leave the bathroom.

"I'll take care of it. Why don't you go and clean yourself up before Daddy gets home?" Ari says without any effort to keep her voice down.

Miss Patty purses her lips, and then turns and walks down the hall away from us without saying anything else.

Ari rolls her eyes when I get closer. "Sorry about that."

"It's okay."

"Every couple of months something sets her off and she gets totally 'faced, and seeing as she's been on this one-thousand-calorie-a-day diet, what she downed this afternoon hit her worse than usual. I think it's all the crap with the park opening and the fact that this new ride we're installing won't be ready and she totally lost it today."

"Oh, that's too bad—about the ride *and* Patty." I hold my phone up and point to Ryan's number, thinking he'll be the perfect excuse to leave. "Um, Ryan tried to call, so I was thinking I should probably see what's going on." I shrug. "You know, before Samantha decides to *entertain* him."

"Yeah, that's cool, but before you call him, I was just wondering if the mirror completely freaked you out."

"How did you . . ." I trail off as Ari bursts out laughing.

"Oh my God, it did, didn't it? I can see it in your face! It's supposed to be like the *latest* in animatronics. My dad paid a freakin' *fortune* for it—for two of them, actually, but once we got them, it was pretty clear we couldn't put them in the park. For kicks we hung one here, and the other is in Patty's office. They're supposed to be the magic mirror—you know, from 'Snow White.' It's totally state-of-the-art voice recognition stuff. You talk to the mirror, and the software analyzes your words and it's supposed to come up with appropriate responses and facial expressions."

"Yeah, I don't know that I'd use the word 'appropriate,'" I say, having a hard time picturing the conversation I'd just overheard being simply computer generated.

"Well, that's what we were told, but as you saw, the mirror isn't really kid friendly. My dad said it was probably a cultural thing—they were made in France and, you know, they do things *a little* differently over there."

I think back to the things the mirror said to Miss Patty. Why would the programmers have even anticipated needing the words "stripper bar" for something geared toward kids? "It was like it was having an actual conversation with Patty—even taunting her."

"Yeah, the software definitely has a few bugs that need to be worked out. Patty gets tanked and starts talking to the stupid thing like the idiot she is, and then gets royally pissed off when it says something inappropriate—which it always does."

"But why didn't you just return them?"

"They wouldn't let us. We even threatened to sue them, but seeing as they're in Europe, they weren't too worried. At least it was a tax write-off."

"Wow, but besides the language, the face in the mirror is a little too PG-13 for the park anyway—it'd give some kid nightmares. They did a really good job on it, otherwise." Totally spooked Remy and me!

"Enough about the stupid mirrors. Nicki's watching *Gypsy*—the Patti LuPone version. Seen it a million times, but if you want, we could head out to the pool. I've got it cranked up to eighty-five!" She cocks her head and looks down at the phone still in my hand. "Unless you're one of those girls who blows off her friends for a guy?"

"No. But I should probably at least call him back just in case it was something important."

"Sure, but before you do, let me show you the pool." Ari leads me to some French doors at the end of the hall, looking out to the backyard.

Large rocks are lit up with soft blue and green lights tracing the path of a waterfall that splashes into the pool. Chinese lanterns hang from cherry trees whose petals drift down onto the pool deck and scatter across the water's surface.

"I could snag some champagne and we could swim or hang out in the Jacuzzi."

"Okay," I say, gawking at the Jacuzzi attached to the pool. "I vote for the Jacuzzi! Let's get Nicki—she'll love this."

"I seriously doubt we could pry her away from the show. And, you know, I'm getting a little tired of her Debbie Downer routine. She takes everything so Goddamn *seriously*. Doesn't she just drive you crazy the way she's always on your case?"

"What do you mean?" I asked, stunned.

"Like riding you about Ryan. I mean, relationships are complicated—you can't just bail on a guy because there's a little trouble, right? But if it were up to Nicki, you'd already be broken up. And having one little drink, what's the big deal? Did you see the way she was glaring at you? It's like she doesn't think you can make up your own mind."

"Well, we kind of are underage, and as far as Ryan goes, she's just concerned that I'm setting myself up for a fall. We didn't know each other too well when he first asked me out—and there's the whole Samantha thing."

Ari looks at me doubtfully. "I guess you could look at it that way, but if you ask me, she's jealous."

I shake my head. "No. Nicki isn't like that."

"Well, I've just never heard her talk about any guys at chorus. Not that Nicki could be bothered talking to me much, even though I've tried to include her in conversations."

I stare out at the pool. Nicki's made it more than clear Ari isn't one of her favorite people, and seeing as Ari can change from hot to subarctic at the drop of a hat, it's not hard to imagine why. But Nicki *has* been riding me about Ryan from the first day he asked me out. I was so excited, but she just stared at me like I was crazy and asked why I said yes to a guy best known around school for scarfing twenty-eight cupcakes in three minutes our sophomore year.

She's only dated a few guys, the longest lasting just over a month. But she's chalked the breakups to the fact that the guys weren't into women's rights or politics or just not—I keep myself from rolling my eyes—*serious* enough.

I guess Ari nailed it.

"But if you want, go ask her to join us," Ari adds.

"No, she'd rather watch the movie. Besides, she thinks bathing suits are designed by chauvinistic people who view woman's bodies as eye candy for men."

Ari shakes her head. "Yeah, like I was saying. But let's get changed, and I'll meet you out here in a few."

Ari heads off and I walk slowly toward the front entrance hall where I left the bag with my suit and towel. I feel a little guilty not coming to Nicki's defense, but in a way Ari's right. Nicki needs to loosen up or at least accept that she's not always right about everything.

I pull my new bikini out of my bag and wish Ryan were here. I'd never admit it to Nicki, but I don't see anything wrong with being eye candy. And maybe next time—if Ari asks me over again—I won't ask Nicki to come.

"So have you gone all the way yet?" Ari asks with a giggle.

I choke on my champagne and then pick up some of the foam gathered at the edge of the hot tub and throw it toward her. "Ari!"

She leers at me. "You're still a virgin, aren't you?"

"That's none of your business!" I squeal, splashing her.

She laughs again. "It's okay, I've never done it either." She sinks a bit lower in the water, the top of her champagne glass tilts and fills with hot tub water.

"Look out!" I laugh.

She sits up and fumbles with her glass, dropping it into the tub. "Shit!"

We laugh some more as we feel around the bottom of the tub with our feet. "I found it," I say, reaching down and grabbing the *flute*—which Ari explained is the proper name for a champagne glass. I explained that we don't do a whole lot of celebrating at my house and therefore I was ignorant to the fact that there was a type of flute you don't blow into. Ari then asked if I could tell a merlot glass from a chardonnay—to which I replied, "No," and she vowed to educate me in the ways of sophistication.

She dumps the water out of her flute and pours more champagne from the second bottle we opened.

"What if Patty or your dad comes out and catches us?"

Ari snorts, dips her lips below the surface, and blows some bubbles. She comes up and crosses her eyes, looking woozy. "Patty's probably out cold." She shakes her head and looks at me sadly. "And my dad is such an old fuddy-duddy he's in bed by nine o'clock sharp." She raises her flute in the air. "This is why it's important to party while you're young and can still enjoy it!"

I raise my glass to hers and then we both sip our drinks. I look up at the sky and marvel at the stars. I went to New York City with Nicki's family a couple of years ago to see *The Lion King* and was shocked that there was so much artificial light it made seeing the stars near impossible. But here, up high on the mountain overlooking the park, each and every star stands out crisply in the black sky.

"It's so beautiful here—perfect."

"I guess," Ari says softly. She swirls a hand across the surface of the water and sighs. "But I'm still missing the key ingredient to my happily ever after."

"Does Luke know you like him?" I ask, not bothering to pretend I don't know she's hot for him.

Ari clucks her tongue. "Sadly for me, he does. I stupidly made the first move and got the you're-like-a-sister-to-me speech. That was over a year ago, and I keep hoping things will change—but it's hard waiting, and seeing him all the time and wondering when he'll realize I'm not a little kid anymore."

"Do you think it's because you were friends with his sister?"

"How did you know Kayla and I were friends?"

"Nicki told me."

Ari nods. "Yeah, I think that may be part of it, but Kayla wasn't much help either. She didn't want us going out because she said if we broke up, it might ruin our friendship. I contended that my marrying Luke would make us sisters." She drains her glass and then fills it again. "Sometimes I think Kayla just didn't want to share him."

I look up at the stars, not sure Ari will like what I'm going to say. I consider keeping my mouth shut, but I do feel bad for her, and the champagne is making me feel brave.

"You might want to back off a little, give him some room. It was kind of obvious you had it bad for him when we were in the costume room that day. Instead of always trying to hook arms with him or stand next to him, which gives off this needy vibe, let him come to you."

I wait to see if Ari's going to bite my head off.

"Maybe you're right," she says.

I realize I'm holding my breath, and exhale.

"Maybe if I turn off the I-love-you vibe then he'll . . ." Ari sits up straight as a huge smile breaks out on her face. "Oh my God, he's here! This is like fate!"

I turn around and see Luke walking out of the house with Nicki.

"Hey, ladies," he says.

"What are you doing here?" Ari says. She looks sideways at me and beams.

"Patty called me a while ago to ask if I finished touching up the sign leading to Hansel and Gretel's forest." He picks at the paint clinging to his hands. "She sounded pretty out of it, so I thought I'd check in on you."

Ari rolls her eyes. "Yeah, she started drinking as soon as she got the call that the new minicoaster is being delayed *again*."

"That's pretty sad," Nicki says. "Are you going to get her some help?"

Ari's smile evaporates. "It doesn't happen all the time," she snaps, then she looks at Luke. "I take it you've met Nicki."

"Oh, I remembered her from the chorus." He turns to Nicki. "I'll never forget that song you sang a couple of years ago—'Glitter' something."

"'Glitter and be Gay,' from *Candide*! That's one of my favorite performance pieces! I can't believe you remembered that." Nicki smiles and waves a hand around like her performance was no big deal, despite the fact that she got a standing ovation.

"No, that song stuck with me for a while. Well, Kayla was singing it a lot too, but she was always talking about how good you were—that you should be on Broadway."

Nicki gives him a bittersweet smile. "She was really good too, but I don't know if I'm ready to take on Broadway."

"Of course you are," Ari says coldly. "Everyone says so,

and you made quite an impression on Luke, who I didn't know was such a music aficionado."

Nicki gives Luke a quick, nervous glance, and I can tell she's realized Ari's heading down that slippery slope of jealousy. "Um, everyone likes music, right? It's universal. Um, you know, it's getting late, and don't you have your big Land of Enchantment orientation tomorrow, Megan? Wouldn't want you to be late for the slushy machine seminar."

I nod and climb out of the hot tub, suddenly self-conscious of being in a bathing suit in front of Luke. I quickly grab my towel and wrap it around me. "Yeah, it's first thing in the morning so we should get going." I wobble a little on my feet, and Nicki grabs my arm to steady me. "There's more champagne, Luke. Maybe you should join Ari." I wink at her and she smiles appreciatively. "Thanks for having us over. Good to see you again, Luke."

"Yeah, you too. I'm sure I'll see you at the park."

I come out of the bathroom clutching my wet bathing suit, and Nicki is leaning against the wall, her arms folded across her chest. "I hope your mother isn't waiting up for you— she'll know you're trashed."

My cheeks burn as I slide the straps of my tote bag over my arm. "I'm not trashed, but my mom has an early meeting with her lawyer so she's probably in bed anyway."

"Whatever, and, uh, thanks for abandoning me tonight."

I scoff. "I just figured you were enjoying the movie, and you even said you weren't sure if you wanted to go swimming."

Nicki takes her keys out of her purse. "It would've been nice to have been asked! After the movie ended I had no clue where you two where. Luckily, Luke showed up and led me to the pool so I wasn't wandering around this flagrantly overdone McMansion filled with butchered-up animal parts.

"Seriously, PETA would be picketing the Land of Enchantment in a heartbeat if they knew what was in here. Just look," she says, pointing to an elephant foot turned into an umbrella stand by the front door. "How sick is *that*?"

I roll my eyes. "It's obviously *old* stuff—from before endangered species were on anyone's radar."

"That doesn't mean they have to keep it around."

"It doesn't, but why get all freaked out about it?"

Nicki opens the front door. "The real question is why are you okay with it?"

"I guess I'm not as morally superior as you are."

Nicki glares at me. "Oh, *that's* nice, and it must be nice knowing you can down as much champagne as you want, seeing as you have a chauffeur to drive you home."

I sigh. "I'm *sorry*, I had a few drinks. It's not like I make a habit of it, but I just don't have the energy to analyze every-thing like you do. Yes, I think all the dead things are creepy, but they're like antiques—maybe there's some sentimental reason for keeping them around."

"Well, FYI, this is my first and last visit to Casa Roy; if you plan on coming again, I suggest you finally get around to getting your license like you keep talking about or have Ari start chauffeuring you around."

"Fine, I will!" I get in the car and wonder when Nicki turned into such an insufferable stick-in-the-mud—or what took me so long to notice. And she's totally delusional if she thinks Ari will ever invite her over again, anyway.

Nicki turns the volume up and I know we'll ride home without talking. It's not fair. She's always harping about stu-pid stuff and she doesn't even know how lucky she is. I'd give anything to go home to a normal family every night and get praise for being great at something like her.

Instead, I'm stuck watching for Remy to pop up around every corner ready to scare the hell out me, and then go to sleep knowing I'll probably have a nightmare about a girl left butchered on a forest floor. I close my eyes, feeling sleepy, and lean my head back against the seat. The face in the mir-ror comes to me. I see its hands clapping, with their long monster fingernails, and pray this image won't be added to my repertoire of nightmares as well.

∿ EIGHT ∿

I walk downstairs and Mom's on the phone. Great. I was hoping she'd be gone by now.

"I'll try to find it, Shelly, but surely in this day and age, you can come up with some loophole—that is what I'm paying you for."

Mom sees me and tilts her head toward the kitchen table, where I see she's laid out breakfast—juice, melon balls, toast—something she hasn't done in ages. I'm guessing Dr. Macardo thought Mom and I should sit down and talk, and this is her way of saying she'd rather just move on instead of rehashing the Remy stuff.

Fergus saunters over and I rub his ears. "Hey, boy," I whisper.

"Look, I just want them to admit they were negligent and have his equipment upgraded." Mom scoffs in frustration at whatever Shelly's just told her. "Well, see what you can dig up before I get there!" She turns off the phone and takes a deep breath.

I sit down and help myself to some toast. I figure Mom is absolutely dying to grill me about the meltdown in Dad's room, but I know she'll avoid it so we can pretend the other night didn't happen.

She pours herself some coffee and runs her fingers through her disheveled hair. "So," she says after taking a sip. "Shelly's trying to have the home take some responsibility for what happened and upgrade all of your father's equipment," she says like I didn't just hear this when she was on the phone a second ago. "And I'm having her talk to the insurance company about doing some more tests—just to see how he's progressing, see if there's any new brain activity the home's missed. It'll be a fight, but . . ." She trails off, sipping her coffee again, and I wonder if deep down she knows it's hopeless.

"Don't forget I'll be home late tonight," she continues. "The competition is in Boston. Fergus and I have been working really hard and I think we have a good shot of beating that Brussels griffon—unless the judges feel sorry for the thing. A dog that ugly could get sympathy points.

There's a bichon frise from Long Island that's getting a lot of buzz on the message boards too. I haven't been able to find any online video of her; it would be nice to see what kind of costumes they have." She rolls her eyes. "Although, I can't for the life of me figure out what attracts people to those yappy little breeds."

"I've got training at Land of Enchantment," I say, not the least bit interested in talking canine freestyle with Mom. Seriously, who cares what ridiculous getup they've put on a small white dog with a bad Afro?

"That's nice." Mom pushes away from the table and puts her mug in the sink. "I might go through some of your father's medical records before I head out to see if I can find something to help our case. I left some money for you on the counter so you can get something to eat tonight."

"Thanks."

She smiles at me, but I don't feel any real emotion behind it. I suspect it was an automatic reaction to my "thanks," and she's already miles away thinking about the competition— and Dad. I watch her go into Dad's study and wonder if she needs to find something that'll fuel her hope that he'll wake up to counteract anything Dr. Macardo may have said to her.

When I talked to Dr. Macardo, despite his efforts to appear unbiased, it was obvious he's not a fan of leaving people hooked up to life support. He must've said, "You have to consider the quality of life," a dozen times, punctuated by "Of course, only the surviving family members can make that judgment call after keeping themselves fully informed about their loved one's condition." I know he was trying to choose his words carefully, but the term "surviving family members" gave him away—he's written Dad off, just like the doctors.

I hear Ryan's car pull into the driveway and honk twice. I give Fergus one last scratch on the head. "Good luck, Fergie, kick some lapdog butt!" I grab my purse and head to the door. "Bye, Mom," I call out. "Good luck!" I count to three but get no response and head out hoping Ari made good on her promise to keep Ryan and me together in the park.

"This is so exciting!" Samantha squeals as we head to the Over the Rainbow Café for our park assignments. "I was looking over our training packet, and I *so* want to do the Mermaid Lagoon boat captain thing. You get to sail around Enchanted Island, and I've even memorized the script just in case they have tryouts or something."

I stare at Samantha in disbelief as she starts reciting the cheesetastic lines.

"While her sisters swam happily in mermaid lagoon, Meriope, the mermaid with long pink hair, longed to play with the children visiting Land of Enchantment. Can anyone find Meriope's hiding spot?"

Samantha pauses, looking around with wide eyes as if she's actually waiting for a boatload of kids to take their fingers out of their noses long enough to spot the fiberglass mermaid hidden in the rocks under the crushing weight of the waterfall.

When we were little, Remy and I always laughed at the poor mermaid statue getting severely pounded by the unnaturally blue water pumped out above her. Once the boat docked at the water park on the other side of the small island, some Land of Enchantment person playing Meriope—complete with the legs our laughter "magically" gave her—greeted us with a Super Soaker water gun. Nothing says "fun" like a mermaid packing heat.

Samantha nods, with a wild smile on her face, and points off to the side of the path. "Yes, you're right, there's Meriope! Wouldn't you like to play with her too?"

Ryan and I exchange looks, and I'm relieved he looks as disturbed as I feel.

"You nailed it, Sam," he says without any enthusiasm.

"It made me wish I was a kid again," I lie, finding it hard to believe she's seventeen and not seven. Of course, she's exactly the kind of person they want working here— Samantha Lee Darling has found a home.

"Really?" she asks.

I nod. "Definitely." Of course, I really want to refer her to Dr. Macardo, because taking the time to memorize such complete drivel is surely a sign of mental illness. Her being the ditz that she is also makes me worry about her ability to safely navigate a boat. I do have to admit I can see the four-and-under crowd totally eating up her schmaltzy performance, though.

"I checked off copilot on my application," Ryan says. "I didn't think I'd be up for the captain spot—it's a little girly."

"Thank God!" I say. "If you'd put in for that, I would've had no choice but to break up. As it is, I'm a little freaked out you signed up for copilot."

"You know I like boats," he says, looking embarrassed.

I raise one eyebrow. "Boats filled with cranky toddlers?"

"Well, no," he says.

Samantha shakes her head. "If you're doing your job right, they won't be cranky. But anyway, I was reading the info packet, and it doesn't take much to get bumped up the salary chain. I'm going to do whatever it takes to make level four and breathe some life into my bank account."

"I don't think you'll have any trouble moving up a level," I add.

"Megan!"

I turn to see Ari booking down a path in a rainbow-striped golf car.

"Hey!" I call out.

She parks the cart and leaps out. "Oh my God, I have to talk to you!"

"Ryan and Samantha, meet Ari—her dad owns the park," I say as she bounds toward us.

"Your dad owns the park?" Samantha asks.

"Sadly, yes," Ari says.

Sam gawks at her. "Seriously? Could you maybe talk to Miss Patty? Because I would do *anything* to get on the Enchanted Island boat captain rotation!" Samantha turns to me and gives me a look like she can't believe her luck. "I even know the part by heart! While her sisters swam happily in mermaid lagoon, Meriope, the mermaid with long pink hair, longed to play with the chil—"

"You don't have to do that," Ari says, holding up a hand in Samantha's face. She stares at Samantha for a second and then blinks twice. "It's more than obvious you'd be *great*, and while I can't make you any promises, I'll see what I can do."

Samantha pumps her fists in the air. "Oh, thank you so much!"

"You're welcome," Ari says. She gives me a sideways glance, and it's obvious she's picked up on the fact that Samantha's completely deranged. "Hi," she says, turning to Ryan and thrusting out a hand. "I've heard so much about you. Do *you* have any requests? Are you dying to be a captain too?"

Ryan shakes his head and blushes a bit. "No. I'm just hoping I get to work with my girls." He puts his arms around me and Samantha, and I could crawl under a rock.

Ari gives Ryan an incredulous look. "How very *Hugh Hefner* of you."

Ryan pulls his arm off Sam's shoulder and starts stuttering. "Oh, no, uh, Sam's just a friend."

"I told you, Samantha's his *best* friend," I say, pretending to be annoyed with her. In reality I'm hoping that if Ryan hears this stuff from someone other than me, it'll finally sink in that keeping Samantha around is not okay.

"Yeah, I think you mentioned that," Ari says. "Hey, do you mind if I steal Megan for a few minutes?"

"Sure," Samantha chirps a little too eagerly.

"I'll catch up to you in a few," I say.

Ari watches them walk away and then gives a low whistle. "She's a piece of work! I definitely don't think you have anything to worry about—I mean, who would go out with someone like that?"

"I think she got dropped on her head as a baby or something—she's totally clueless, but there isn't a mean bone in her body," I concede.

"Well, I'm sure she'll have a nice time cleaning up after

the baby goats. I've got her spending the afternoons in the Fun Farm."

I feel torn. On one hand, it'd be fun hearing Samantha complain about the shit factor in the farmyard, though there's a good chance the baby animal cuteness will trump crap for her. On the other hand, she'd be 100 percent better at the boat captain gig than, say, the Goth girl I saw walking toward the café a few minutes ago. I mean what was Mr. Roy thinking when he hired *her*?

"You know, Ari, Samantha really *would* like to do the mermaid thing. Seriously, she's memorized the whole speech, and as sad and pathetic as that is, she recited it to us and did a really good job."

Ari raises an eyebrow. "Are you sure? You're being awfully nice to the girl who's just waiting to get her sugarcoated claws into your man."

"Yeah, I'm sure. Besides, she's exactly the kind of person your father would want leading the way to Meriope's hideaway."

Ari shrugs. "Okay, I have you and Ryan on the other side of the park running rides in the Forest section—the log flume, Hansel and Gretel's, and the Gingerbread Coaster. Hmm. I'll need someone to take Samantha's place in the farm, though. Hey, you!" Ari stops an exceedingly tall brunette walking by. "What's your name?"

The girl looks down at Ari. "Yohanna," she says with some sort of thick European accent.

"Do you like animals, Yohanna?"

She gives Ari a puzzled look. "An-ee-mals? Yez," she says with a shrug.

"Fabulous!" Ari walks over to her golf cart and takes a clipboard off the passenger seat. "Can you please spell your first and last name for me, *Yohanna*?" Ari says, imitating her accent.

The girl narrows her eyes. "J-O-H-A-N-N-A. L-U-N-D. Any-ting else?"

Ari scribbles on her clipboard and then looks up at Johanna. "Nope, I'm good, thanks. You're gonna *love* the goats."

The girl stalks off toward the café, and Ari puts the clipboard back in the cart. "Some of these foreign exchange students need to learn their place big-time. I mean, they think we'll fall all over them just because they have an accent. Enough of that, though, because I have been *dying* to tell you what happened last night after you left!"

"What?"

"Luke happened! I did just what you said. I was *totally* cool—like I didn't care if he stayed or not—*and he stayed*! He got in the hot tub with me, and even though I was dying to get right up next to him, I kept away and we just hung out and it was like old times—you know, before I told him I liked him and things got weird."

I smile, but a part of me is bothered that Luke got in the hot tub with her. Another part of me wants to slap myself on the wrist for caring.

"We talked about him going to art school in New York City. I said I thought he should take his time getting his portfolio together. You know, so basically we can *both* go *next* year—but I didn't say *that*." She sighs, her face looking peaceful and happy. "I think we may be back on track."

"That's great!" I say, but my gut tells me she may be reading more into it than she should have.

She beams and claps her hands—a very Samantha move. Man, she's got it bad. I'm glad Ari's feeling over-the-moon happy, though, because if Ari's happy, everyone is happy. "Hey, I was wondering if you wanted to join me for a spa date? We can get a mani-pedi and a massage."

"That sounds great, but I don't think I have the cash for something like that."

"It's my treat—payback for helping with Luke."

"You don't owe me anything," I say, thinking I really didn't do anything massage worthy.

"Well, we'll just do it for fun then," she says. "I won't take no for an answer!"

I smile. "Okay, I've always wondered what getting a massage would be like."

"It's heaven! I'd better switch Yohanna and Samantha on the schedule before Patty hands it out." She rubs her hands together and gives an evil laugh. "I love messing with the employees!" She grins. "This summer is going to be the best ever!" Ari gets back into her cart and waves as she drives it around the back of the café.

The hairs on the back of my neck stand out as a cool chill comes over me. Remy comes into view, hazy and unfocused. "Meggy, where's Daddy?" she asks dejectedly as she walks slowly up the path.

She looks so forlorn, and tears come to my eyes because I can't help her. "I'm trying to find him for you."

"Where's Daddy?" she asks again, her voice cracking. She bows her head and shakes it back and forth. "Make a wish." She catches her breath and sobs. "Make a wish."

"Hey!"

I jump and turn to see Luke. I rub my hands across my eyes and wait for my heartbeat to return to normal.

"Sorry, I didn't mean to spook you. I figured your sister had that covered." He points in Remy's direction. "She's stage two right now—transparent but visible."

I raise my eyebrows.

"I'm learning ghost lingo, but I was hoping we could

talk." He looks around and tilts his head away from the café. "Do you have a minute?"

I look back at Remy fading as she keeps shaking her head and muttering. I nod and follow him up the path. He takes a turn toward the Giant's Sky Garden—an area filled with metal flowers and bugs the size of cars.

"Over here," he says, ducking under a red speckled mushroom. There's an opening in the mushroom's stem and I follow him inside.

He sits on the curved bench lining the interior and I slide in next to him. We're definitely out of sight, but I can't help worrying that Ryan or Ari might somehow discover us.

"Okay, I've been talking to Nona about Remy."

"You have?" I ask, my voice echoing in the hollow mushroom. "But won't she get suspicious?"

Luke takes a deep breath. "I told her about me, and she didn't seem too surprised. I think she's probably always known, but that's not important."

My heart melts knowing he outed himself just to help me. "That must've been hard."

"Well, after you left, I got to thinking—thinking that for every person who comes to see Nona because they want otherworldly advice about their wardrobe, there are people like you who really need help . . . and Remy's just a kid, and what kind of a creep would I be if I didn't help her?"

"Nona could've done it."

"Yeah, I know, but Remy came to me that day in the costume shop." He sighs. "And since I've spent all of my life trying to know as little as possible about the ghost business, I knew I'd need help. So I told Nona we thought Remy was looking for your dad—and what that situation is—and that the key to Remy moving on lies with your mom, who can't see her."

Luke looks up into the top of the mushroom and I say what he won't. "And Remy can't find my dad unless my mother agrees to pull the feeding tube."

"Right," he says, reaching out and squeezing my hand. I take in that momentary rush of peace and catch my breath as he lets it go.

I hate to admit it, but I wish my hand was still in his. I shake my head. Concentrate on Remy!

"My mom, she won't do it," I say, staring out into the oversize garden, feeling small and hopeless. "I told her I thought it might be time to let him go and she flipped out—called me a murderer."

Luke shakes his head. "You know that's not true."

I shrug. "I don't know. I really don't. One minute I think it's the right thing to do, but then . . . well, if anything, my bringing the subject up has made her more adamant than ever to prove that he *will* wake up. She's even going through his old records, trying to find anything to force the insurance company to order a bunch of new tests."

"But if she can *see* Remy, she might change her mind."

"Yeah, but she can't."

Luke looks me in the eye. "But I might be able to help her see Remy—even talk to her."

My mouth slowly opens. "Are you serious?"

Luke frowns. "Nona says I can, but it's not like I've ever *done* it before. It's worth a try, right?"

"But what about Nona, can't she come to my house?"

Luke shakes his head. "I asked, but she said this is *my* job."

I look at him imploringly. "But Nona said she'd never turn anyone down!"

"She doesn't feel like you're being turned down, because like it or not, you have me."

"Okay," I say, picturing the look on Mom's face when she sees I've been telling the truth about Remy all along. "If Nona says you can, I believe her. So when do you think we should do it? As soon as possible?"

He furrows his brow. "I was thinking we may not want to start with your mom. If I can't pull it off, you'll just be in a worse mess than you already are."

"True."

"So we need to find someone else to practice with—someone Remy was close with."

"Nicki," I say quietly, wondering if she'll even speak to me after what happened at Ari's. "Nicki was Remy's best friend. But Nicki doesn't believe in ghosts; she's just about as antighost as you can get."

Luke smiles. "Then she'll be perfect. If we can make *her* believe—make her see Remy—your mom will be a piece of cake."

"Okay, I'll call her after this stupid training session. Can you do it tonight?"

"Yeah, and we should probably do it at your house, where Remy will feel more comfortable, to up our chances she'll show herself."

"Great. My mom'll be home late—she's got a dog competition in Boston."

"She's showing your dog?"

I roll my eyes. "No, dancing with him—I'll tell you all the embarrassing details later." I hand Luke my phone. "Punch in your number and I'll call you as soon as I get in touch with Nicki."

He hands me my phone back and I shake my head. "I don't know how I can thank you for everything."

"I'm doing this for Remy—and for you."

My cheeks burn, and I look down at my watch. "I'd, uh,

better get going, the meeting's already started."

"Yeah, you wouldn't want to miss the enchanted team cheer."

My eyes widen. "Oh, God, there's a cheer?"

Luke stands up. "Who's got the magic? Who's got the smile? Who's got the vision to go the extra mile? Land of Enchantment, that's our name—happily ever afters, that's our game!"

I stare at him, looking for a sign that was a big joke. "Please, please, tell me you made that up?"

"Nope. The whole darn enchanted team gets in a circle every day before opening and does the cheer, then Patty runs around high-fiving everyone."

As if on cue I hear Miss Patty's voice on a loudspeaker. "Who's got the magic?"

I let out a long sigh. "Are you coming to the meeting?"

"Nope, I'm an *unofficial* level four team member—meaning I have access to restricted stuff and rides but don't have to do the cheer." He looks me up and down. "I may be wrong, but I'm guessing team-building cheers aren't your thing."

"This whole park isn't my thing."

"Who's got the smile?" blares through the air.

"You better get going."

I start jogging back to the café. "Who's gonna make a fool of herself for the rest of the summer?" I mutter. "Go, Megan!"

⌒ NINE ⌒

I race down the path to the Over the Rainbow Café, and when I enter, everyone's in a circle just like Luke described. I see Ryan and Samantha and wedge myself between them.

"You missed the cheer," Samantha says, holding out her hand for Miss Patty.

"I heard it," I say as Miss Patty slaps my hand on her way around the circle. She doesn't make eye contact with me, and I figure she's embarrassed about last night.

"Did I miss anything important?"

"Not much," Ryan says. "She went over the different areas of the park. Unless you get food or gift shop assignments, we'll be trained on three attractions to start with and can put in for new assignments after a few weeks."

"Do you think that girl will be able to get me the boat job?" Samantha asks.

"Ari?" I nod. "Yeah, she said she'd do it."

Samantha beams, and I can't help thinking she'd be perfect to take over Miss Patty's job when she retires.

"Okay," Miss Patty booms through her microphone. "Before you get your assignment packets, there are just a few last pieces of business.

"Character actors should report to Ye Olde Costume Shoppe at one to meet with our very own Henrietta Stupin, who is back for her *fifteenth* year playing our very own Mother Goose!"

Miss Patty puts a hand above her eyes and scans the crowd. She stops and points to what looks like a one-hundred-and-ten-year-old woman. "Henrietta, can you give all our team members a wave?"

Henrietta gives a halfhearted wave, and everyone claps, though I'm not sure walking around in a park with a stuffed goose for fifteen years is anything to celebrate.

Miss Patty winks at Henrietta. "Isn't she just adorable? We're so *lucky* to have her back, and maybe some of you will be like Henrietta and make Land of Enchantment your forever home too!"

Henrietta smiles thinly, and maybe I'm wrong, but

she doesn't look terribly excited about having Land of Enchantment as her forever home. Who can blame her? I certainly wouldn't want to try to entertain kids who probably know more about Pokémon than Mother Goose.

"Okay, before you get your packets, my dear ol' hubby, aka, Mr. Land of Enchantment himself, would like to say a few words. Let's give a great big enchanted cheer to show him how excited we are to get this season started! *Who's got the magic?*"

"Who's got the magic," I say halfheartedly, turning my head to save my eardrum from being shattered by Samantha's enthusiastic replies.

"*Who's got the smile?*" Patty claps her hands and everyone joins in.

For every person rolling his or her eyes, there are five or more who seem to be enjoying this as much as Samantha. What is wrong with these people? I wonder. Then again, I should've expected this. You'd have to be crazy like Samantha—or desperate like me—to work here. Who knows, maybe Samantha will find a kindred spirit among the losers cheering their heads off.

"*Who's got the vision to go the extra mile? Land of Enchantment, that's our name—happily ever afters, that's our game! Go team! Go!* And let's give a big ol' hand for Mr. Roy!"

I notice Ryan clapping just as hard as Samantha and hope he's just being polite.

Mr. Roy walks up to the podium and dabs his eyes with a bright pink hankie. He looks out at us with his hands clasped at his chest.

"This is what it's all about. Your *enthusiasm*, your caring about *dreams*, and your desire to *transform lives*. My family has been running this park since 1934, and who would've guessed we'd come this far and make so many people happy? But we can't do it without you and your dedication to happily ever afters, and I thank you from the bottom of my heart!"

We clap some more and Samantha sticks her fingers in her mouth and whistles.

"I ask only one thing of you," Mr. Roy continues. "Let your smile light the way for a family in need of cheer and give them the chance to escape the harsh realities of life. Thank you, one and all, for being a part of my enchanted family."

Mr. Roy bows his head and dabs his eyes again to wild applause. I find myself clapping along, wondering if Luke will be the key to my happily ever after. My stomach turns nervously. Ari said almost the same thing about Luke last night. But I'm talking about Remy not romance. Still, I shiver thinking about how wonderful it feels being with him, even if it is just about Remy.

God, why do I feel guilty just thinking about Luke

Amador? I reach out and take Ryan's hand to ground myself in reality. He leans in and kisses my cheek.

"Hey, what are you doing tonight?" he whispers as he wraps his arms around me.

"Um, Nicki's coming over."

He nuzzles the back of my neck. "I was hoping I could come over."

Guilt wells up in me. "I really can't blow her off, but at least we're still on for tomorrow, right?" I hate that I'm lying to him, but seeing as I can't explain why Luke will also be there, I really don't have a choice.

"Yup, I made us dinner reservations at the White Mountain Hotel." He grins expectantly, and I feel guiltier than ever.

On our first date we hiked the White Horse Ledges and had lunch on a cliff overlooking the hotel. I told him I'd heard how great the restaurant was and wanted to go there someday. And he remembered.

"I thought I should take you someplace special for our one-month anniversary."

I pull away from him. "That's *tomorrow*?"

He looks hurt. "Yeah, I thought girls kept track of those things."

"Ha, yeah, well, there's just been so much going on. I can't wait, though!"

"Me too," he says, taking me in his arms again.

"Hey!" Samantha says. "Didn't you read the no-PDA rule in the employee manual?"

I turn and kiss Ryan hard on the lips. "Guess I missed that one, but thanks for the heads-up!"

Miss Patty takes the microphone from Mr. Roy and stands behind the row of boxes on a table near the front of the café. "Your schedules are here in alphabetical order, so come on up, and then let's get to work!"

Samantha races ahead and I say a silent thank-you to Ari for pulling strings behind the scene so Samantha will be on one side of the park and Ryan and I will be on the other!

"So now that you've all had a chance to try out the operations board on this ride," says Kevin, our level-four enchanted instructor, "I need to emphasize again that accidents can happen if you access this or any other ride without following the marked safety paths. *Stay on the paths!* This is one of the oldest rides in the park, and not following procedures can result in serious injuries, including loss of limb, and even fatalities."

Ryan and I exchange looks. Hansel and Gretel's has just gotten a heck of a lot scarier.

"So, any questions?" Kevin asks.

Sarah Franklin, who goes to school with us, raises her hand. "Is it too late to switch to food services?" she asks, looking very pale. Given that she fell in one of the log flume boats while practicing using a squeegee to wipe the water off the seats, and pinched her fingers while closing a safety bar on the Gingerbread Coaster, this warning of death and dismemberment is apparently a deal breaker.

Kevin flips some papers on his clipboard, pulls out a red card, writes her name, and then signs his at the bottom. "Take this to Miss Patty. It's the equivalent of a panic button—just give it to her and she'll see to it that you're reassigned."

Sarah snatches the card and scurries down the path.

"Anyone else not feeling up to this?" Kevin asks.

I look around at the seven other people left in our group and we all shake our heads.

"Good! So let's do a run through." Kevin looks at our name tags. "Izzy, why don't you take the control board at the Witch's oven? Hayden, you take the exit board. Izzy, don't forget you have to push the alert button once each car dips under the oven. Hayden, when you see the light flash, you'll know you have a car to unload in one minute, so be ready. Seamus, you load passengers. The rest of you can take a ride, and then we'll switch."

"After you," Ryan says as we walk to the entrance.

We wind our way through the queue, and Seamus picks up the microphone.

"Welcome-to-the-haunted-forest-please-read-the-safety-precautions-and-note-this-ride-may-be-too-intense-for-children-under-the-age-of-ten," he says rapidly in an Irish accent.

"Seamus," Kevin calls out. "Slow it down, and it's under the age of five!"

"Oh, sorry," Seamus says into the microphone. "Under the age of *five*."

I push through the turnstile, and Seamus lowers the mic and smiles. "Please-keep-your-hands-and-feet-in-the-car—"

"Slower!" Kevin barks.

"And remain seated at all times. If the ride should come to an unexpected stop, uh, please stay in your car until an enchanted team member can assist you."

I get in the cupcake-shaped car and Ryan slides in next to me. Seamus pushes the safety bar down on our laps, bites his lip, and looks around as if not sure what to do next.

"Release the brake," Ryan whispers to him.

"Oh, thanks!" Seamus steps on the brake release, and then pushes a button on the starter board. "Enjoy the ride."

The cupcake car jerks forward, and we inch slowly toward a door painted like the inside of an old cottage. The door opens and a menacing voice calls out from above. *"Take them into the forest and leave them there!"*

The car winds its way through trees covered with hanging moss. Owls flap their wings and hoot as their red eyes blink. A tree branch cracks and drops dangerously close to our heads. I duck down and snuggle in closer to Ryan. A wolf springs out at us, howling, and I scream.

"I don't think that wolf was working last time I was in here," I say, trying to laugh.

Ryan puts an arm around me. "Yeah, I don't remember that."

A trio of vultures sitting in a tree screeches at us, jerks their heads around, and follows us as the car turns sharply around a boulder. A cloud of bats dips down from the ceiling and circle overhead.

"There's the gingerbread cottage," Ryan says as the car rounds another corner.

"Good!" I say. I think I liked this ride a lot better when most of the animatronics were broken.

An old hag with a long, crooked nose stands to the side of the door, beckoning to us. "Come in for some tasty treats, kiddies," she says over and over again. I remember how much I hate the next part. The inside of the witch's house is at all sorts of crazy angles, with the floor tilting up toward the giant flaming oven.

The front door opens and the car zigzags wildly around the kitchen table laden with oversize cakes and cookies, and then past a large cage with a Hansel robot shaking the bars as he calls out for his sister. We head toward the oven, fake flames spitting and crackling, and then the witch slides across our path and the car jerks to a stop.

"Into the oven with you!" the witch's tinny voice shrieks, her red eyes flashing just like the owls', but then Gretel slides toward the witch, and the car moves forward. The oven door opens and I hear Izzy call out to us.

"In ya go, guys!" she says, imitating the witch's voice.

I turn my head and see Izzy wave to us from her hiding spot behind the pantry loaded with more fake cookies and treats. The witch skates on her track into the oven, which lifts up into the air, exposing the sharp incline the car will go down. My screams echo along with the witch's as the car dips sharply.

Ryan laughs and squeezes me tighter. Hot air is pumped over us as red strobe lights flash along the "fire"-covered walls. The car streaks down until we come to the door at the back of the oven. It opens and we're in a forest scene again, only this time the mood is cheerier. Bluebirds chirp on branches and flutter their mechanical wings, fawns drinking from a babbling brook lift their heads as we roll by, and gentle Bavarian music fills the air.

Hansel and Gretel skate on a path along the back wall like they're racing home for a happy reunion with their father, who is waiting on the front porch of their rickety cottage.

I can't help thinking Nicki was right. This is a really messed-up ride.

"Well, we didn't get cooked at least," Ryan says. He picks up my hand and kisses it.

I lean my head on his shoulder, thinking this is the last time I plan on taking a spin in the old cupcake cars. Suddenly Remy appears—standing directly in our path, shaking her head.

"Don't come back here, Meggy," she says.

The car goes right through her and I'm hit with a blast of cold air.

"Whoa," Ryan says, shivering. "Did you feel that?"

I turn around in the car and see Remy staring after us. "This is a bad place!" she screams. "Bad! She's here—*right under here*. They're gonna get her too. She's gonna die!"

"Who?" I whisper.

"What?" Ryan says.

"Help her!" Remy cries.

The car bursts through the last door, and Remy's screams echo after us. Hayden's eyes lock onto mine. The car comes to a halt, and Kevin comes running over. "*Hayden!* You didn't hit the brake lock!" he yells.

Hayden quickly pushes down the lock and shakes his head "Sorry! It's Megan, she looked—"

"I don't care what she looks like!" Kevin barks. "When the car comes to a stop, you lock the brake until it's time to send it to the loading dock!"

Hayden turns bright red. "Sorry."

"We can't afford even one mistake, do you hear me? Do you think you can get a grip or do you need a red card too? I hear the custodial crew loves having new recruits handle the urinal cake replacements."

"I can do this," he says quietly.

Ryan and I hop out of the car, and Hayden can't stop stealing glances at me. Is it that obvious something is wrong with me?

A beep comes from the exit panel. Hayden stands at attention, and I'm pretty sure he won't forget the lock this time.

"Jeez!" Casey Winters says as her car comes to a halt at the exit. She jumps out, looking wildly around. "Some idiot was yelling, 'She's gonna die,' in there! It totally freaked me out!"

Oh my God, she heard Remy!

She glares at us, but we all shake our heads.

"She's nuts!" Tyler Michaels says as he slides out of the same car. He rolls his eyes. "I sure as hell didn't hear anything."

"Hey!" Kevin yells. "Watch the language! You'll get fired

in a heartbeat if anyone hears you talking like that once we're open."

Tyler scowls. "Sorry."

Izzy walks out of the staff entrance and looks quizzically at all of us. "Everything okay?"

Casey shakes her head. "Was that you yelling in the ride?"

Izzy nods. "I called out as you passed by."

"No!" Casey says. "The 'she's gonna die' crap?"

Izzy's eyes pop. "I didn't say anything like that, I swear."

Casey's lip trembles. "Well, I don't care what anyone says, I heard it, and I'm not going in there again! I want one of those red cards." She holds out her hand to Kevin.

Kevin rubs his eyes for a second and then pulls a card off his clipboard and starts writing on it. "I don't know why they keep this ride—there's something about it that gets to people," he says as he gives it to her. "I have to transfer at least five kids a year out of this one."

As Casey walks away, she looks back over her shoulder one more time, and then quickens her pace. Nothing like a little Remy fun to make a creepy ride even creepier.

Kevin exhales loudly. "I fucking hate training day," he mutters.

Tyler lets out a snort. "Nice talk from a level four," he says under his breath.

"Okay, people!" Kevin says, clapping his hands and smiling like that will clear away the pall hanging in the air. I half expect him to start up the Land of Enchantment cheer. "Do you think we can finish this up so we can go home?"

We all nod, but everyone looks a little nervous now.

"Great! Megan, you take the oven; Ryan, you'll do the exit; and Tyler, you load. Let's hustle!"

I so don't want to go back in there. But it's only Remy; no need to be more afraid than usual. Well, except for the "she's gonna die" part.

"You okay, babe?" Ryan asks, and I realize I'm just staring at the staff passageway into the ride. "Do you want to switch with me?"

I shake my head. "Um, no, I'm good. Casey got me a little spooked, that's all. It's just a ride though, right?"

"Yeah." Ryan takes a quick look around. Kevin is explaining something to Tyler, and he leans in and kisses me. "Are you sure?"

I nod.

"Okay, see you in a few."

I hope so. And I hope Remy was just talking about the girl she already showed me and not . . . I shake my head. I don't even want to think about the possibilities.

ᓚ TEN ᓗ

I duck through the passageway under the STAFF ONLY sign and drag my hand along the dark walls. A few dim bulbs every few feet light the way, and I keep my eyes on the glow tape lining the path. The walkway opens up a bit onto the Haunted Forest. The wolf jumps out to my right and I suck in my breath. It howls frantically and I wrinkle my nose. Who the hell designed this ride? No doubt the same nuts who made those mirrors.

Just keep going, get to the cottage, check in two cars, and then get out of here.

I walk up the steps and hear the witch's voice punctuated by the sound of Remy crying.

Fabulous.

The path narrows and I start climbing the stairs to reach the control panel.

"Meggy," she whines.

I look up and see Remy at the top of the metal stairs.

"Go away, Remy!"

"Meggy, she's gonna die."

"*Who* is gonna die?"

Remy's face crumples. "Where's Daddy?"

"God, I don't have time for this!" I walk right through her, shivering in the wake of cold air around her.

I march up to the control board and hit the speaker button. "All set," I say, my voice higher than normal.

I ignore Remy and look around the witch's house. The jarring angles and too-bright candy-colored pinks and purples make my head spin. I look at the Hansel robot shaking his bars and fumble for my inhaler. I exhale and put it to my lips, but Seamus's car enters the house before I can use it. I wait until the witch slides out and push the button to alert Ryan.

Seamus is clutching the safety bar, and I remember he's one of the exchange students, so he's never been on any of the rides here. "Watch out, the track's gonna drop!" I call out, trying to keep my mind off of Remy's nonstop rant.

"Thanks!" he yells as his car dives beneath the oven.

A few minutes later, the car carrying Hayden and Izzy comes into the house. They're laughing, oblivious to Remy's tantrum. Hayden points to Hansel in the cage. "Someone put a muzzle on that kid!"

"Hell," Izzy says, "I'll throw him in the oven just to make him shut up!"

I push the button when they're at the oven, and then Remy appears in front of me completely solid, her face contorted in anger. In the back of my mind I take a second to wonder what stage Luke would call this.

"Why won't you listen?" she says slowly. Water starts to drip down her forehead and gather at the ends of her braids. Her hands ball up and she glares at me angrily. *"Why won't you help her?"*

Izzy and Hayden whoop it up as the oven lifts and their car careens down the slope.

"Stop laughing!" Remy shrieks. The electric board sparks up, and then the power goes out.

I drop my inhaler and freeze in place as Hansel's frantic cries become slow and distorted and finally fade to silence. Smoke fills my nostrils and I pray the board won't catch on fire.

"Helloooooo?" Izzy calls out, laughing from inside the oven tunnel. "I think we're having *technical difficulties.*"

"Here, witchy witch," Hayden bellows.

"Shut up!" Izzy says, but she's laughing.

I stare at the place where I think the board is, relieved there aren't any flames.

Izzy starts the Land of Enchantment cheer. "Who's got the magic? Who's got the style?"

"It's *smile*," Hayden cuts in.

"Who cares? Who's got the vision to go the extra mile? Land of Enchantment, that's our name—*crappily* ever afters, that's our game!"

One of them proceeds to make farting noises and they both erupt in giggles.

"I have to get out of here," I whisper. I stand up and feel my way along the wall. An icy chills passes me and I hiss at Remy. "This is your fault!"

I feel her small cold hand take mine, and then I'm in the woods. Real woods—not the fake one inside the ride. Someone crashes through the brush, breathing heavily. *"Oh my God, just leave me alone!"* a voice shrieks.

Who is it? Izzy and Hayden are making so much noise, I can't get a good read on the voice.

"Please!"

A second person passes about six feet from me, picking their way carefully but quickly through the brush. I see a glint of sliver in the moonlight—a knife.

"Leave me alone! Somebody help me! Help me!"

I try to listen to the voice but Remy is screaming and Izzy and Hayden are yelling out the cheer again.

There's a jumble of noises—snapped branches, *Land*

of Enchantment, leaves crunching, *save her*—and then a scream cut short. I listen for more, but all I can hear is Hayden and Izzy. At least Remy is quiet now. But then there's something else. A sound. A repetitive sound. All I can think of is the sound the knife makes when my mother carves the turkey on Thanksgiving and she hits the bone and cartilage. Grating.

It's getting harder to breathe, and I feel around the wall, trying to retrace my steps back to the control board to find my inhaler. I hit my shin on something and curse. And then the lights are back on. Hansel is crying for his sister and I'm gasping for air.

Ryan comes running toward me. "Megan! Are you all right?"

I put my hand on my throat. "Inhaler," I wheeze. "Dropped it."

I grab onto the control panel to steady myself, but I know I'm going to pass out. I feel the inhaler pass between my lips and the medicine pumped into my mouth. I gasp and choke but instinctively hold my breath and count to ten in my head. Then I slowly exhale and my breathing eases.

"Here, sit down," Ryan says as he helps me into the chair. The power flickers off again, and I clutch his arm.

"Don't leave me," I gasp.

"I won't," he says, holding me tight and stroking my hair. He moves the inhaler into my hand, knowing I'll need another hit.

Then I hear Remy again, but this time it's soft, hiccupy sobbing like she always does after one of her big meltdowns.

A flashlight pierces the darkness. "Megan?"

"Luke!" I call out. "We're over here!"

Luke flashes the light over Ryan and me. In the dim beam I see a look of surprise on his face. "*Oh!* I didn't know someone was with you."

I nod. "Yeah, this is Ryan."

"Do you two know each other?" Ryan asks stiffly.

I nod again. "Luke works here, and he's a friend of Ari's."

Luke is looking back and forth between Ryan and me, and I'm suddenly uncomfortable. I hear Samantha's voice in my head—*No PDA, it's against the rules*—and untangle myself from Ryan.

"Um," Luke begins, "the generator is acting wonky, so I told Kevin I'd get you and he's going in through the back exit to get the people stuck in the tunnel. And"—he looks at Ryan—"you'd better not let Kevin see you leave; you're not authorized to come in during a shut-down."

"*Sorry*, I didn't want to leave my *girlfriend* in the dark!"

Luke turns on another flashlight and hands it to Ryan.

"I just don't want you to get in trouble, that's all."

"Let's get out of here, Meg," Ryan says, holding out his hand and pulling me up.

Luke stands aside and lets Ryan go first. "Wait," he whispers as I walk by. When Ryan rounds the corner, Luke puts a hand on my shoulder and leans down close to my ear. "What happened? I heard her clear across the park."

I start walking. "Another vision is what happened—another scary-ass vision!" Tears well up in my eyes. "We've got to do it tonight, with or without Nicki. I don't care if we have to pull a random stranger off the street!"

"What about your *boyfriend*?"

"No, not him," I say, and hurry to catch up with Ryan. As I walk carefully in the light Luke is shining my way, I wonder, why not Ryan? He certainly seems less skeptical than Nicki. But Nicki was Remy's friend. Surely she'd be more likely to show herself to Nicki. I nod. Nicki's the one.

As we make it closer to the exit, I can see the path outside in bright light and a crowd gathered around Miss Patty.

"Okay, team," Miss Patty says. "We called you over so you can see how to handle things in an emergency. If a ride goes off-line, what's the first thing you do?"

People look at their feet, but one hand shoots up from the crowd.

"You in the back!"

Samantha steps forward. "You try the backup generator and then immediately alert whoever is on supervisor duty for your area of the park!"

Miss Patty smiles at her. "Right you are! Good job! And who goes in to help anyone stuck on a ride?"

"Only level-three or-four employees," says a tall, skinny guy with a French accent standing next to Samantha.

"Excellent!"

They lean into each other and Samantha blushes. Dare I hope Samantha might be hooking up with a French hottie?

"Don't worry people," Hayden says loudly as he leads Izzy and Kevin out of the exit. "We were this close to being baked in the witch's oven, but we kept our heads, remembered our enchanted team training, and made it out alive with only one finger being chopped off!" He holds up his hand with his thumb hidden in his palm.

People start laughing and clapping, but Kevin waves his hands in the air.

"Whoa, whoa! No one lost a finger, and there was never any danger of anyone not making it out alive," he says, glaring at Hayden for a second. "But this was a good drill and I'm proud of the way *most* of my team handled it. Now, if your team leader says you're done, you can head on home. Don't forget, character actors still have to meet in the costume shop."

Luke gives Ryan a sideways look. "Later," he says. "I've got to get back to work."

Samantha waves to the French guy and then skips over to Ryan and me. "Oh my God! I can't believe you were trapped in there, Megan. Were you scared?"

"No," I lie, "but Ryan here did come to my rescue." I hold up my inhaler.

He gives me a quick squeeze and then takes a step away, obeying the no-PDA rule.

"Well, I'm really glad I'll be out in the open air! I'm doing the captain gig for the SS *Mermaid*, the swan boats, and the water fun park. And I met this supernice guy, Christophe from *France*, who'll be my second mate. And I think he might like me!"

"A French second mate? You lucked out," I say, thinking Christophe from France just might signal the end of the third wheel in my relationship.

"I know!" she chirps.

"Well, just be careful, Sam," Ryan says. "You've know him for what—a couple of hours? And he's from France!"

"What's wrong with *France*?" I ask, glad I didn't tell them about the messed-up export from said country hanging on the wall at Ari's.

He shrugs. "It's France—*no one* likes France. And what happens when he goes back there at the end of the summer?"

Samantha frowns.

"Hey, that's a long way away," I say, giving Samantha a conspiratorial smile. "*And* there's nothing wrong with a summer fling."

Samantha sticks her tongue out at Ryan. "Exactly! And I don't even know if he *likes me* likes me."

"It sure looked like it to me!" I say.

"My team!" Kevin barks. "Over here!"

"I'll wait at the benches," Samantha says.

Ryan and I walk over to Kevin, who's looking more stressed-out than ever. "Okay, I just talked with Miss Patty. This ride is closed until further notice. It'll need an electrician to go over the wiring, then it's gotta be inspected." He shakes his head. "It's one of the oldest rides and it's always causing trouble."

"So do we need to get trained on another ride?" Izzy asks.

"No," Kevin says. "Until this is up again, we'll have you relieve people during their breaks. Some of you will be on cleanup, and some will get a quick gift shop orientation. Anyone a character actor?"

I raise my hand.

"Megan, you may get some extra hours at that until Hansel and Gretel's is fixed."

I nod. For once I'm glad I signed up for the Snow White gig.

"We'll have your new schedule printed when you show up on opening day," Kevin says. "I apologize for the inconvenience." He waves dismissively at us and turns toward the office building shaking his head. "I hate training day and I hate this fucking ride."

Ryan and I look at each other with wide eyes as Tyler stares after Kevin and says, "*He said it again!* Why did he jump all over my ass? I only said 'hell.'"

"You need to be at least a level three to swear," I say.

Tyler rolls his eyes. "This is such a crock of shit. *Who's got the magic?*" he says bitterly. "Crock of shit," he says again after giving us a wave good-bye.

"I've got my costume meeting, hopefully it won't take too long," I say after Tyler leaves.

"I can't wait to see you dressed up as Snow White," Ryan says.

"Wouldn't you rather see me undressed?"

A smile breaks out on his face. "Yes! Can't you tell Nicki you have more training tonight?"

Reality crashes in again. "I wish I could." I truly mean it too, because I know Nicki is not going to like being a guinea pig for Luke's ghost wrangling.

"Oh my God! Look!" Samantha yells, running toward us with her phone held out in front of her. "I just got a text message from Christophe. He asked if I wanted to hang out tonight! There's a softball game at the exchange students' dorm!" She jumps up and down a few times and I raise a hand to give her a high five, which she eagerly hits.

Ryan's brow furrows. "You're not going are you?"

"Of course I am!" She giggles as she starts to text Christophe back.

I give Ryan a puzzled look. "Why wouldn't she?"

"She'll be with a bunch of strangers."

"She's a big girl," I say, though I can kind of see why he'd be worried. Samantha is the antithesis of street smart. "And I read in the information packet that there's supervision at these things—she'll be chaperoned."

Samantha puts her hands on her hips. "Who says I *want* to be chaperoned?"

"It's just better that way, until you get to know the guy," Ryan says.

"And I better head off to the meeting," I say, not liking the look on Ryan's face, and not liking the nagging suspicion that he's not as happy as I am that Samantha may be moving on to foreign pastures. "Why don't you see if you can find Christophe while I'm there?"

Ryan looks at me with his eyebrows raised, but I don't care—I'm determined to see a Samantha/Christophe hookup.

Samantha squeals. "Oh, great idea!" She takes her phone out and starts pecking away at the tiny keyboard.

"I'll wait by the front entrance—alone," Ryan says. "Like tonight."

I keep myself from rolling my eyes. "Hopefully the meeting won't be too long, and we can hang out for a bit afterward." I wink at him and he smiles, making me feel like an utter creep for lying.

~ ELEVEN ~

I walk into Ye Olde Costume Shoppe and see Miss Patty
has already started. She looks up at me. The smile in her
eyes is gone and I wonder if she'll demote me to the Fun
Farm despite whatever strings Ari has pulled.

"Sorry I'm late," I say quietly, and then make my way to
the back of a crowd of at least thirty people.

"As I was *saying*, being a character actor is just about
the most important job in the Land of Enchantment world.
Once you don one of these finely crafted costumes that I
have painstakingly made sure are accurate to the tiniest
detail, you become that character, and you become one of
our *Faces of Enchantment*."

Faces of Enchantment? In the illustrious words of my

coworker Tyler, *what a crock of shit.* I'm half tempted to raise my hand and ask what about Bo Peep's ultrashort miniskirt is historically accurate? Or should I mention the Snow White look-alike I saw had a much more detailed bodice? Sure it was soaked in blood, but still, it was a hell of a lot nicer than the satin Halloween knockoff I'll be wearing.

I shake my head. I'm officially losing it. How else can I casually compare my outfit to what some poor girl lying butchered on the forest floor was wearing?

Oh!

What if that horror show I just saw was the chase *before* the kill? I hear the sound of the knife cutting through bone in my head, and my stomach turns. God, she was hunted down like an *animal.* Bile rises in my throat and I swallow it down.

"Are you okay?"

I jump and see the girl staring at me.

"Maybe you should sit down. You look like you're gonna pass out," she whispers.

I take a deep breath. "I just need something to eat. I haven't had lunch."

She nods but moves a couple of feet away from me as if what I've got is contagious—or maybe she's afraid I'll throw up on her or something. One thing's for sure, it's getting harder and harder to pretend everything's fine, and people are starting to notice the cracks in my facade.

I just pray Luke can successfully work his psychic mojo on Nicki tonight, and then we can try it on Mom.

My heart sinks. In order for Remy to move on, then Dad's got to too. As much as I keep thinking it's for the best, what if I'm wrong and Mom's right?

Tears gather in my eyes and I try to brush them away without looking too obvious. It's hard to believe everything was status quo just a few days ago, and now Remy's turned everything upside down.

"I have about a million things to do before opening day, so Henrietta is going to give you a few tips about being one of our Faces of Enchantment," Patty says as she smiles and waves her fingers around her face.

"Oh, and would Megan Sones please come to my office afterward?"

I stand up straight, totally taken off guard. "Um, sure."

After Patty leaves, Henrietta Stupin gets off her chair and looks at us wearily. "First thing you need to know is ya gotta marry rich or invest wisely so you don't get stuck schlepping around a park in your eighties like me. Second, and you returning girls already know this, putting on one of these hoochie-girl costumes brings out the worst in even some of the biggest churchgoing men, so you'd best be keeping an eye on roaming hands."

A few people titter, but we mostly just stare at her.

Henrietta gives one girl sitting on the floor the evil eye. "Don't think it'll happen to you, eh? Well, I'm in my eighties and I got my rear end slapped *sixteen times* last summer, and some old coot got a little too friendly with my bra while I was posing with him and his granddaughter and he knocked the padding out of the left cup! I ain't got nothing without the padding neither."

She looks around at us, nodding her head. "So just imagine how many'll hit on you young things!"

I exchange horrified looks with the girl next to me. She's looking a little faint herself now, and I'm pretty sure this is not the talk Miss Patty envisioned.

"And don't try and turn 'em in either," she continues, "'cause they'll just deny it and call you crazy. Trust me, I know! And as for you boys who signed up for Prince Charming, get a life!"

The five guys in the room all flush deeply, but the rest of us laugh.

"Hey, I'm the Big Bad Wolf," one pimply guy says, looking around at the rest of us, but no one says a word.

Henrietta puts her hands on her hips and looks around the room. "Any questions?"

Everyone's head shakes.

"Good! Don't know why Patty wanted me to talk to you anyway. You dress up and walk around—what's to know?"

She rolls her eyes. "Class dismissed 'cause I gotta get a smoke!" Henrietta salutes us and stalks out of the room.

"Too bad we can't at least get tips for being groped," one girl says as we start to file out of the room after Henrietta.

I hang a left down the hall to Miss Patty's and wonder if I'm going to be fired for being late for the character meeting, or for seeing her trashed the night before.

As I approach Miss Patty's office, the door is open and I hear her singing. I recognize the song from the CD of chorus selections Nicki was playing in her car on the way to Ari's—"Someone to Watch Over Me." While her voice is not as polished as Nicki's, Patty conveys the longing in the words much better. Given what I know about the Roy family, it's no surprise she has the emotional baggage to give the words more depth.

I feel weird walking in midsong, but with Ryan waiting I want to get this over with. Plus, I still need to get in touch with Nicki so Luke can play ghost whisperer on her.

I give Patty another minute, but when she starts over from the beginning of the song, I knock on the doorjamb. "Um, sorry, but you said you wanted to see me?"

Miss Patty jumps. "Oh," she says, bringing a hand to her heart. "You startled me."

I grimace. "Sorry, you were singing and . . ."

Her faces flushes under the thin line of hot pink powder she's brushed on her cheekbones. "Just me making more of a fool of myself than I already have." She looks away and it's obvious she didn't call me in to fire me. She's embarrassed about last night.

She motions for me to sit on the pink polka-dotted chair in front of her desk.

"No," I say sinking into the overstuffed pillows. "You're really good. You should be in the chorus with Ari."

Her eyes widen in surprise. "Me? No! I mean, I love to sing, but I don't think Ari would enjoy having her mother watching over her, if you get my drift."

I nod. "Yeah, but you do sing really well."

She gives me a genuinely pleased smile. "It was these little ol' pipes of mine that first caught Mr. Roy's attention. He heard me singing in a club down in New Orleans and bought me a drink afterward. The rest is history."

I can't help thinking the real story of their meeting sounds a bit classier than what the mirror said the night before. I so didn't want to think about Mr. Roy stuffing twenties in her G-string at a stripper bar.

"Anyway, I asked you to come by so I could apologize for my behavior last night. You were a guest in my home and I was not the hostess I should've been."

Now I'm embarrassed. What do I say? *No worries—*

my mom trash talks with mirrors after she's been binge drinking too.

"Um, it's okay."

"It's not okay, and you're showing me more kindness than I deserve. I just hope you can find it in your heart not to mention yesterday's events to the other team members. If not for me, then for Mr. Roy and Ari—they shouldn't be punished for my lapse in judgment."

"Oh, I won't say anything—I never planned to. I understand, you know, that stuff happens."

Tears well up in her eyes. "You're a good kid. I knew it the minute you walked into my office, and I . . ." She pauses and furrows her brow. "I know you and Ari are getting to be friends." She smiles but it seems forced. "Ari doesn't have many friends, besides Luke, and well, I probably shouldn't be saying this, but—"

"Patty!" Kevin rushes into her office. "Henrietta fell. I think she may have broken her hip! We called 911, but you'd better come see her."

"Oh, crap!" Patty says, pushing her desk chair back. "Please tell me it wasn't—"

Kevin purses his lips and nods. "Yeah, that sidewalk we haven't repaired yet."

Patty grabs her cell phone and hustles around the desk. "You call Mr. Roy, and I'll call the lawyers." She looks at me as if she'd forgotten I was there. "Oh, thank you for coming, Megan, I really do appreciate it!"

They dash out of the office, and I exhale. That was close! Of course, being fired wouldn't have been the end of the world—especially in light of Christophe being thrown into my mess of a love triangle. I stand up and catch my reflection in the gilded mirror hanging on the wall. I look over my shoulder and then walk behind Miss Patty's desk.

I brush my dark bangs to the side. I really could use some sun this summer—my skin is so white, I practically glow under the fluorescent lights in the office. Hopefully, Hansel and Gretel's will stay broken all summer. There are definitely more chances to be out and catch some rays at the roller coaster and log flume, and frankly, I don't ever want to go near that witch's house again!

I run my hands up the sides of the mirror, trying to feel the on switch. I can't find anything, and I'm not about to lift it away from the wall—with my luck it'd come crashing down. I run my fingers around the carved frame one more time. Those people in France did a great job making it look old.

I take a chance and go with the obvious. "Mirror, mirror, on the wall, who's the fairest of them all?"

The mirror shimmers and I catch my breath. I remember that it's voice activated, and as my reflection vanishes and the dark face comes into view, I take a step back, thinking I should've just run out to meet Ryan by the exit.

"You were once most fair, 'tis true, but now . . ." the face begins, and then its eyes widen. "You!"

I stare at the face. "Me?" I choke out.

The face's expression softens. It smirks. "*This* is a *most* interesting development."

Remy appears at my side, her eyes as wide as saucers. "*No, Meggy!* Don't talk to it. It's bad."

I shake my head. "I *do not* have any energy left to deal with you! Can't you see it's not real?"

"It's bad, Meggy," she says, shaking her head. "I need Daddy—he'll fix it. Where's Daddy?"

My heart starts to pound. "Just stop it and leave me the hell alone!"

Remy rocks on her heels, looking aimlessly around the room. "But if you make a wish . . . yes, that'll help. Star light, star bright, first star—"

"*Oh my God! It's a toy—it's not real!*"

"A ghost!" the mirror says.

Ghost? My blood freezes. "What did you say?"

The glass shimmers, and my reflection reappears, looking wild and crazed. "*What did you say?*" I scream at the mirror, wondering if this face—this wild face I'm seeing—is what got Hayden so freaked he forgot to lock the brake earlier.

"It's gone," Remy says with a sigh. "It's gone."

She fades a bit, and I step closer to the mirror. *"What did you say?"* I repeat slowly, carefully pronouncing each word.

Nothing happens, and I shake my head. "You don't have to say it again, I heard you the first time."

I wait for a minute for the face to come back and then I roll my eyes and turn away. I'm talking to the mirror like Patty was. Might as well get "nut job" tattooed on my forehead. "God, I'm crazy," I whisper. "I'm really crazy."

"Bad," Remy says, her voice hushed like mine.

"No, I told you, it's a toy," I say, but I can't help thinking that no matter how carefully that thing was programmed, the chances of it saying, "Ghost," with Remy in the room are astronomical.

Remy walks through me. Chills wrack my body. "She's gonna die," she says matter-of-factly. "Die."

My heart rockets in my chest. I run out of Miss Patty's office and head for the exit. I burst through the door and find a bench to sit on. I exhale slowly and take out my phone. I bring up my call list and punch in Nicki's number.

By the fifth ring I start to wonder if she's so mad she won't pick up.

"What?" she says, and I'm so happy she answered, tears prick my eyes.

"Nicki? Can you come over tonight? I really, really need to talk to you." She doesn't say anything and my heart starts to pound again. "Nicki? Please."

"What, is Ari too busy drinking bubbly in the pool?"

"I don't know what Ari's doing, but I'm sorry about last night, I was a total jerk."

"Go on."

I'm about to completely lose it. I've been through hell the last few days and now I have to suck up to Nicki just to get her to talk to me. I take another deep breath. It's not Nicki's fault Remy is haunting me, but if all goes well, she'll be a heck of a lot more sympathetic.

"And I don't want any time to go by without us talking it out. I want things to be okay with us."

I hear Nicki clicking her tongue in her mouth—something she does when she's trying to make a decision. "I want that too," she says quietly.

Relief washes over me. I feel guilty that I'm not telling her the truth, but right now I'd sell my soul if I thought it'd solve my Remy problem.

"So you'll come over? Say around seven?"

"Sure, whatever," she says and hangs up.

She's still mad, but at least she's coming over. I scroll through my contact list and stop at Luke's number.

"Megan?" he says, picking up on the first ring.

"Yeah, we're on—seven o'clock. My house is at forty-two Ivy Way."

"I'll see you at seven."

"Good, because you're my last hope, Luke. If this doesn't work, I'm voluntarily committing myself and asking for heavy sedation."

"Megan, what happened?"

"You know that vision I showed you—the girl?"

"Yeah."

"Remy showed me the *events* leading up to it, and I . . . I heard the knife cutting through her."

"Oh, God."

My shoulders shake as my face contorts. Tears flow and I can't speak.

"Megan? Are you still there?"

I take in a jagged breath. "Why is she doing this, and h-how am I supposed to act like nothing's wrong? If it weren't for you, I'd feel like I was losing my mind."

"We'll fix this," he says with such confidence I almost believe him. "But if Ari calls you, don't tell her I'm coming over. I had kind of a weird conversation with her yesterday after you left."

I sniff. "I won't say anything. And thanks. I don't know what I'd do without you."

"Good thing you don't have to worry about that."

I put the phone in my purse and take out my compact. God, I look like crap. I brush some powder on my red nose and head for the parking lot. I look up at Rapunzel's tower, the one Luke added the extra touches to.

Here's hoping Luke will be my knight in shining armor.

⌒ TWELVE ⌒

Nicki looks back and forth between Luke and me with one eyebrow arched high. "Okay, so which one of you is gonna say, 'April Fools,' so we can all have a big laugh, and then I can go home?"

I guess I'm not surprised by her reaction. I'd probably say the same thing if I were her. Luke reaches out, squeezes my hand, and nods for me to keep going. "This isn't a joke," I say calmly. "We're *totally* serious and we really need you to help us."

Nicki puts her hands out in front of her. "Just stop right there; I've been *more* than tolerant with you and your boyfriend drama, but using me to test-drive Luke's ghost-hunting prowess on *Remy* isn't even remotely funny. And honestly, if for some reason you actually do think Remy is wandering around haunting things, you need a serious reality check and a full refund from Dr. Macardo."

Luke and I exchange looks. He pulls on the knees of his jeans nervously. I'd warned him she was going to be tough, but even so, I'm getting mad.

"You want a reality check?" I say. "How about accepting the fact that you could possibly be wrong about something? Just because *you* don't want to believe in ghosts, doesn't mean they don't exist. I know this all sounds crazy, but—"

"No, it doesn't *sound* crazy, it *is* crazy," Nicki interrupts. "And if I'd had any idea you were planning on ambushing me with *ghost boy* here, I would've called your shrink myself. Not that your sessions seem to be working real well, but maybe you two can get a group rate or something."

"Hey!" Luke says. "This isn't an ambush, this is about helping Megan and Remy. All we're asking is for you to have an open mind."

Nicki glares at Luke. "*Open mind? Are you for real?* You ask me over here under false pretenses, and then think I'll gladly sit around some freaking crystal ball so you can test your ghost-hunting ability on me? There are meds for this stuff, you know!"

Luke shuffles his feet. "Actually, I'm not really trained to use a crystal ball yet; I was going for more of a conduit kind of scenario."

I hang my head. I knew things might go badly, but not this bad.

"Oh my God!" Nicki laughs crazily. "Here's a novel idea: Why don't you guys call your good friend *Ari* and see if *she* wants to play haunted house, because I'm not interested!"

"Nicki," I say quietly, trying to stay calm, "it has to be you. She'll come to you—you were Remy's best friend."

"That's right!" she yells. "And if Remy was really here, she would've come to me!"

"*That's* why you didn't believe me in second grade, isn't it?"

"No!" she says, but the look on her face says otherwise. "I didn't believe you because people don't come back from the dead!"

"Nicki, Remy didn't come back—*she never left*. She showed up right after the accident, and she'd pop up every now and then over the years. But lately she's been showing up more and more, and if you could see her, you'd know she needs help. We think she's waiting for my dad to, you know, so she can move on to *wherever*. But unless we can make my mom see her, too, it's not gonna happen."

Nicki stares at me for a second, then rolls her eyes. "I'm outta here!" She stands up to leave, but Luke rushes over to her and takes her hand. "Let go of me!" She starts to pull away, but then her shoulders relax and she turns to him.

I know Luke's working his empath mojo on her, and I hold my breath, waiting to see if he can break through the wall she's put up.

"We're telling you the truth—we need your help," he says slowly. "I know you're feeling conflicted, but I also know a part of you wants to believe us. Even if you think we're crazy, what harm is there in humoring us?" He pauses. "Remy would've come to you if she could," he says quietly. "The ghost world isn't like ours. They're dealing with the past, present, and future all at once, and reaching out to even one person is hard. Megan's her *twin*."

Nicki's face screws up, and then she looks at the ceiling. "Remy's *gone*."

Tears streak down my cheeks. "She should be, but she *isn't*. Please, Nicki, help me. Help Remy."

Nicki purses her lips. Luke leads her back to the couch. "Just let me try it—that's all I'm asking."

I cautiously sit next to Nicki. She's breathing hard and I tentatively put an arm around her shoulder. She leans into me and I burst into tears because I know she'll stay. "Thank you."

Nicki nods against my shoulder and I look at Luke with wide, teary eyes, not sure what to do next.

He takes a deep breath. "Okay, um, this is the first time I've tried this, so bear with me. And we, uh, need to be linked." He reaches out for Nicki's hand again.

Nicki stiffens for a second but lets him take her hand, and then I feel her relax.

"I'm going to call her, and if we can get her to appear, I'll, um, well, I'll try to pass the sight on to you, Nicki. My grandmother said if we both concentrate, you should be able to see her."

Nicki scoffs. "When this doesn't work I want you two to get some help."

"It'll work," I say. It has to.

"Open your mind to the possibility—believe it can happen," Luke tells her. He clears his throat. "*Remy?* It's me, Luke. There's someone who wants to see you. Are you here, Remy?"

I scan the room, but there's no sign of her.

"Remy?" he calls again.

"Remy?" I echo.

Please let this work.

"Remy, Nicki's here. She misses you," he continues.

Nicki sobs and slides an arm around my waist.

I look around the room—nothing. I look over Nicki to Luke. *Where is she?* I mouth to him.

"Nicki, what did you and Remy like to do?" Luke asks.

"I don't know. We'd play with Megan, and . . . I don't know."

"The shows," I say. Remy inherited Dad's smooth singing voice, and she and Nicki were always putting on shows. They'd let me rehearse with them, but when it came time to perform for our parents, I was always demoted to ticket taker/usher. "Nicki, what if you sing to her? What's one of the old songs?"

Nicki shakes her head. "You gotta be kidding me if you think I'm gonna sing right now!"

My brain scrambles, trying to remember a song—any song. "*Remy?* Do you want to *sing* with Nicki? You can put on a show."

I catch my breath as Remy appears, soft and unfocused near the fireplace. "There," I whisper, pointing. "Do you see her?"

Luke squeezes Nicki's hand, and she sits up. "No. This is so stupid, this . . ." She cuts herself off and leans forward, staring at the fireplace.

"That's it," Luke says. "You're looking right at her."

"He likes to dance," I sing a bit off-key. "In the Bahamas."

"In his pajamas," Nicki sings in a whisper, her eyes wide, staring ahead.

I struggle to come up with the next line. "The island life is so fair."

"*You could see his underwear,*" Remy sings, and then

giggles. She walks toward us—right through the coffee table. "A show!" she says, smiling from ear to ear. "We should charge a dollar this time."

I catch my breath. "*Do you see her?* Can you hear that?"

Nicki takes her arm out from around me and reaches toward Remy. "Oh my God, yes. Braids, purple dress. I can't believe it."

Remy takes a step closer, and the air around us ices up.

Nicki stretches forward as if trying to see whether Remy's solid to the touch. Her fingers pass through her and she gasps, no doubt feeling the intense cold that forever wraps itself around my sister. "*Remy? It's me, Nicki.*" Her body shudders, wracked with tears. "Remy."

"Nicki's here," Luke says. "Remy, try to see her, she's right next to Megan."

Remy cocks her head, and then her eyes open wide. *"Nicki!"* She smiles for a second, and then her face clouds over. Her features sharpen, coming clearly into view. *"Nicki! Don't go there! It's bad! Make a wish, Meggy, make a wish. No, Nicki, no!"*

Remy trembles and turns to me. "Meggy, it's bad. She's gonna die. You've gotta help her! *You gotta help her!*" Water starts to drip from the hem of her dress.

Nicki turns to me, her eyes as frightened as Remy's. "Wh-what is she doing? What's the matter with her?"

Oh, shit. I hoped Remy wouldn't slip into panic mode with Nicki! I even convinced Luke not to warn Nicki about Remy's out-of-control tantrums so she'd be more open to this whole thing.

"Remy, calm down," I say. "We'll put on a show, we'll sing more songs!"

"No!" Remy says, starting to rock on her heels. She shakes her head and I hear the water from the river splash and roar by—just like the day of the accident. *"Bad! Bad! Daddy'll help. She's gonna die."*

"What's wrong?" Nicki yells. She jerks her head around the room. "What's that? The water noise?"

Luke drops Nicki's hand and stands up. *"Remy, it's okay,* Nicki's okay."

"Daddy, help her!"

Suddenly the door opens and Fergus trots in. He looks at Remy and his tail drops down between his legs. He barks twice in her direction.

Remy scowls and shakes a finger at him. "Bad dog," she says as she disappears from view.

Mom follows him in, shutting the door behind her. "We won! We beat that little troll of a Brussels griffon and the bichon too!"

Nicki, Luke, and I are frozen in our spots as Mom stares at us.

"H-hi, Mom, that's great," I say, knowing it's obvious Nicki and I have been crying and she'll be wondering why.

Mom puts her purse on a chair and walks slowly over, eyeing us suspiciously. "Is everything okay?"

Nicki looks at me, her eyes about to pop.

"Ha, yeah, Mom, of course everything's okay. We were, uh, just watching a show, and it was intense. So intense, we had to turn it off."

"Oh," she says, still giving us the eyeball. "Are you going to introduce me to your friend?"

"Huh?" My head whips around to look at Luke and then back to Mom. "Oh!" I force a smile on my face and hope I don't look as crazed as I feel and that Mom won't notice the puddle of river water Remy left behind on the floor either. "This is Luke, he works at Land of Enchantment painting scenery and stuff."

He takes a few steps toward Mom and holds out his hand. "Nice to meet you." He shakes her hand and his brow furrows. "That's funny, you look really familiar."

Mom smiles. "I *was* featured in the entertainment section of the *Conway Daily Sun* not too long ago with Fergus here." She reaches down and scratches Fergus behind his ears. "We do canine freestyle—it's a combination of obedience training and dance to show off the bond between a dog and his handler."

Luke shakes his head. "Um, I don't think I saw that, but maybe . . ." His eyes flash with recognition. "Did you have an appointment with my grandmother this morning?"

Mom raises her eyebrows, looking puzzled. "Your grandmother?"

"Amador's Psychic . . ." he starts to say, but he looks at Mom's horrified expression and stops. "Maybe it was the article."

Mom's face reddens. "Oh, well, actually I was there, but it was nothing." She smiles broadly. "The White Mountain Freestyle Club is having a raffle and I was"—she brushes the side of her nose and looks away from me—"soliciting businesses for raffle donations." She nods her head. "I got a gift certificate. To raffle off."

She bobs her head up and down a few more times, and it's so obvious she's lying. "I'm going to get my things. Wait until you see the trophy we won. It's so big I had to get help getting it into the car." She turns abruptly and heads out the door.

Nicki flops onto the couch and buries her face in her hands. "Oh. My. Freaking. God!"

I jump up and rush to Luke. "My mother was at your house? Do you know what this means?"

His eyes light up and I know he's thinking the same thing I am—she was there asking questions about Remy!

"She believes you," he says. "Or—"

"Or wants to," I say, finishing his sentence.

"People!" Nicki snaps. "Can we please talk about what just happened instead of whether or not your mother got a psychic consultation along with her freaking gift certificate?"

"Sorry," I say. "I was just thinking her visiting Luke's was a good sign."

"A very good sign!" Luke adds. "If I explain the circumstances, maybe Nona will tell me what went on."

"Oh my God, that would be great, and it would totally help us figure out the next step, and—"

"People!" Nicki yells again.

I turn to see Nicki staring at us in utmost disbelief, her jaw clenched in anger. "You brought me here to test out Luke's *ghost power*—which, to be really honest, I'm wishing hadn't worked—and now you're acting like I'm not even *here*!"

Fresh tears tumble down Nicki's cheeks and I feel like an absolute creep.

"Why was Remy all freaked out?" Nicki asks. "Why did she say those things?"

I sit down next to Nicki and take her hands. "I don't know why Remy said those things, but she's being doing this a lot lately and that's why we're trying to help her move on."

Nicki's right eye twitches. "I think that's a very good idea."

I wrap my arms around her. "I'm sorry we didn't warn you, but I thought if you knew how bad Remy was, you'd never agree to be our guinea pig."

Nicki lets out a short sob. "Yeah, you're right about that, but I'm sorry too. Sorry I didn't believe you, and that you've had to face this alone all these years."

Mom starts kicking the front door and Luke runs over and opens it. She walks in with two bags hanging over her shoulder, struggling with a trophy that's at least four feet tall.

"Here, let me help you." Luke grabs the trophy and she drops the bags to the floor.

She puffs out her cheeks and exhales loudly. "Thanks! Is this to die for or what?" she asks, pointing to the trophy.

After hearing Remy's rant, the "to die for" reference is taking on a different meaning for us. I'm also thinking the trophy is just a hunk of craptacular plastic, but we all smile appreciatively at it. What else can we do?

Mom pats the gold figures of a dog and a person. "Meg, would you mind taking this to the trophy room? I'm wiped out and need to get cleaned up and ready for bed. And it's late, you two, I think it's probably time to head home."

Nicki nods. "I'll come over in the morning so we can

talk some more." She looks at me with such pain in her eyes, I feel guilty I brought her into this mess.

"Okay."

"Do you need a ride?" Luke asks Nicki.

"You know, even though my house is just a block away, walking in the dark doesn't sound very appealing right now."

Luke takes his keys out of his pocket. "I'll call you," he says to me.

"Okay. And, Luke, thanks."

"No problem."

When the door shuts, I walk over and pick up the trophy with a grunt. It's a lot heavier than it looks.

"Can you manage it?" Mom asks.

"Sure thing," I say, chipper as always in the face of unnerving Remy stuff.

I hoist it up, lean it against my shoulder, and head to the trophy room. Ten years ago that was Dad's office. His stuff is still there, but a lot of it has been pushed aside and boxed up in a corner to make way for all the freestyle crap Mom's accumulated over the years.

It's ironic that she can tenaciously hang on to the hope that Dad will wake up but at the same time totally take over his space. And this was his space—he made it clear the study was "Daddy's room." But maybe the trophy room is where Mom can be honest with herself, even if she can't admit it.

I flip on the light and take in the room. Most of Dad's nonfiction books, the ones about raising chickens and organic gardening—for the farm he dreamed about retiring to—are shoved aside to make room for the trophies that dominate the shelves.

The desk is where it's always been, complete with family photo. I pick up the picture and look at our smiling faces. Remy and me with matching braids and outfits. It feels like a lifetime ago.

I grunt again and hoist the trophy up onto the desk. I see a file labeled MEDICAL INFO on the desk. It must be the one Mom was going through this morning.

I open the folder and look at a page of incomprehensible MRI results. Why can't they put this stuff in terms we can all understand?

I shake my head and turn the report over. The next page is blood work results. I continue flipping through pages, and my heart revs up as I see one labeled ADVANCE DIRECTIVES.

If I, Jim Sones, should have an incurable or
irreversible condition with no hope for recovery,
I choose the following:

I scan the rest of the page.

—tube feeding *No*

—antibiotics for infections *No*

—being transferred to a hospital for treatment *No*

—artificial nutrition *No*

—hydration *No*

—pain medication *Yes*

Oh my God! She knew he wouldn't want to be hooked up to all those machines, but she did it anyway. All these years Remy has been waiting for Dad because Mom refused to honor his wishes!

I snatch the paper up and storm back into the family room.

"*Mom?*"

"Upstairs!"

I race up the stairs to her room.

"How could you do it?" I ask, thrusting the paper at her.

She peers down at the paper, and I'm stunned when she looks back up at me calmly. "Because there's always hope."

"Hope? It's been ten years! I've read the research and I know you have too. The longer someone is in a persistent vegetative state, the less their chances are of ever recovering!"

Mom sits on her bed. "But there's still a chance. I love your father and I'm not about to give up on him."

"This isn't about giving up on him; it's about the fact that all this time you've had a will that clearly states Dad wouldn't have wanted to live like this—if you can even call it living. Have you looked at him lately? Really looked at him? Do you honestly believe he would have wanted this?

"And what about Remy? What did Mrs. Amador tell you about her? And don't bother denying that's why you really went there."

Mom looks away from me and breathes deeply. "Mrs. Amador said Remy was looking for something." A tear rolls down her cheek.

I sit down on the bed next to her and hold the living will in front of her. "She's looking for Dad. You need to do the right thing for both of them."

"I just *can't*, Megan." Her shoulders shake, and part of me wants to hug her, but it's been years since we've embraced and I can't bring myself to do it.

"Remy's in a lot of pain, Mom. She needs Daddy."

Mom gets up, walks to her dresser, and pulls a few tissues out of the box.

"Promise me you'll think about it, okay?" I ask.

She nods and I stand up.

"I thought I heard her yesterday—after you left."

I freeze. "What?"

"I was combing my hair and thought I heard Remy reciting the star light, star bright poem. Remember you used to say that at night, the two of you?"

My heart pounds. "Oh my God, Mom, that was Remy. It *was* her—you heard her! You *have* to believe me now."

I look at Mom, red nosed and clutching the tissue. I hold my breath.

"That's why I went to the Amadors'," she says. "I thought I was going crazy, but you seemed so adamant that she was really here. I had to find out." She shakes her head. "Mrs. Amador couldn't get her to appear, though." Her face crumples into tears.

I sit back on her bed. "Remy was with me today—at the park."

Mom sits next to me and clutches my hands tightly. "Why can't I see her?"

"You can. Luke can help you." I hold out my arms. She leans into me sobbing, and we're hugging for the first time in years.

"Megan, I'm sorry," she whispers. "I think I've always known Remy was still here, but I just couldn't bare the thought of my little baby not being at peace. I couldn't face it, and I ended up hurting you in the process, and I'm so, so sorry."

She cries harder, and I hug her tighter. "There's only one way for her to be at peace."

Mom nods, and for the first time, I feel hopeful this nightmare might finally be ending.

⟳ THIRTEEN ⟲

Oh my God, she heard her?" Nicki asks, and then she blows on her coffee. "So that means she believes you about Remy, right?"

I take a bite of the cinnamon bagel Nicki brought over this morning and wiggle my toes under Fergus, who's curled up on the floor below me. "It looks that way, and she didn't even threaten to send me to Dr. Macardo. Really, there's no other explanation for the weird things that have happened over the years. I actually have to give her credit for holding out so long. I mean, how do you explain pictures and knickknacks launching themselves across the room if not for a ghost?"

Nicki nods. "I'm having a hard time imagining anyone rationalizing that."

"According to my mother, we've had a lot of earthquakes over the years, but maybe hearing Remy and knowing all the weird shit happened despite the absence of seismic activity made it easier to believe. Luke thought that since Remy's totally agitated about things, she's using more energy to make contact and that's what made it possible for my mom to hear her. Someone at Land of Enchantment did too. I doubt that girl will set foot in Hansel and Gretel's Haunted Forest ever again."

Nicki lets out a long breath. "This is all just so mind-blowing—first Remy and now the will. How are you keeping it together? I mean, I only saw Remy once and I'm still shaken—I hardly slept at all. I kept hearing her shouting, 'She's gonna die,' over and over in my head."

"I don't have a choice. At least the 'she's gonna die' stuff happened a long time ago, maybe even at the site where Land of Enchantment is now. The day of my interview Remy *showed* me the victim, and after that it's been one freak-out after another with her."

Nicki looks sick and covers her mouth. "Oh, God."

"I'll spare you the details."

"Thanks, but do you think Remy's going to keep at it until she can be with your dad?"

"That's what I'm thinking."

"Would a judge uphold the will if your mom was fighting it?"

"I think so. I stayed up late and read about a lot of similar cases online. If there's a will, the hospitals have to honor it or pay a kick-ass settlement when they get sued."

"Wow. This is a lot to process!" Nicki sits up and faces me on the couch. "Let's move on to something a bit cheerier, shall we? What's the deal with you and Luke?"

I look at her with her eyebrows raised expectantly. "There's no deal, he's helping me with Remy."

"Uh, that's not the feeling I got last night."

"What do you mean?"

"Well, when he drove me home he asked how long you and Ryan have been going out. He tried to make it sound like he was just making conversation, but it's so obvious the guy is hot for you, and I was just wondering if it's mutual."

My cheeks redden. "He doesn't, and it isn't. But . . ."

"But?"

I sigh. I so didn't want to go here, not after all of the complaining I've done about Samantha. "Okay, if I'm being completely honest, I have been kinda thinking about him a lot. I keep telling myself it was just because he's helping me with Remy, but . . ."

"But?"

"But he sends shivers up my spine every time he touches me." I bury my face in my hands. "I'm really, really confused."

Nicki laughs and I look up. She gives me a sly smile and an I-knew-it look. "The really confusing thing is why your boyfriend hangs around with a girl who's made it abundantly clear she's in love with him. If Ryan is serious about you, he should've cut Samantha loose a long time ago. As it is, he's leading her on, and frankly, it's kinda cruel."

"Actually, Samantha hooked up with a Land of Enchantment exchange student from France yesterday." The squirmy feeling I got when Ryan tried to shoot down Samantha's budding romance with Christophe returns.

Nicki scoffs. "That doesn't change the fact that Ryan's been a complete dickhead about the whole thing."

I nod. "You're right, and I hate to admit it, but it was pretty obvious he wasn't happy about her hooking up." My shoulders slump. "Seriously, you should've seen him—he kept trying to talk her out of it and warning her about the evils of France."

Nicki's lip curls up. "See, this is what I'm talking about! It's beyond ridiculous to put up with that crap."

"To be fair, I don't think he truly gets why it's a problem, and he tried really hard to make things up to me the other night. He brought over movies and Chinese, and yesterday he told me he got us dinner reservations at the White Mountain Hotel to celebrate our one-month anniversary tonight. I know he cares, and I care about him too. It's just that, no matter what, Samantha is hovering all the time."

"And there's Luke."

I hang my head.

"Look," Nicki continues. "I'm not saying Ryan doesn't care; obviously he chose you over Samantha. But do you really need a guy who comes with his own *groupie*? Why get all angsty about it if there's someone *else* who sends shivers down your spine?"

"But how do I know what I'm feeling for Luke isn't just a result of the empath stuff?"

Nicki hunches her shoulders. "Huh?"

"His family, they're empaths—you know, they can take away your pain, make you feel better just with a touch."

Nicki smiles and holds out her hand. "Well, ghost boy held this hand last night, and there were no shivers running up and down my spine. Don't get me wrong—he's totally cute, and I definitely felt more relaxed every time he touched me, but there were no shivers, not even a tiny goose bump. Well, maybe there were some goose bumps after Remy appeared, but they had nothing to do with Luke."

I sink back into the couch cushions and stare at the ceiling. "Yeah, well, Luke has a groupie too—Ari. She's totally in love with him, and there's no way I could go out with him even if I wanted to—which I'm not saying I do—because I can't go against the girlfriend code."

Nicki blows a raspberry. "You've known Ari all of a week; the code does not apply."

"It does! Ari's told me how much she likes him—I can't pull a Samantha on her."

"Stop hanging around with Ari and it won't be an issue! Seriously, the girl's a head case. You should've seen her glaring at me the last chorus practice. If you want to invoke the girlfriend code, then how about you show some loyalty to your best friend—*moi*—and dump her princess ass!"

"I know you two don't see eye to eye, but I do like her. She went out of her way to make sure Ryan and I would be working together, and she even got Samantha assigned to her favorite ride in the park—all just because I asked her to. And then there's the spa date she made for the two of us next week." I wasn't planning on mentioning that to Nicki, but I feel like I have to explain why I can't just dump Ari.

Nicki rolls her eyes. "Well, then we have no choice but to send a letter to the pope and have her nominated for sainthood. I can see it now—Ari Roy, patron saint of amusement parks and French manicures."

"Ha, ha. She doesn't have a lot of friends and she's just trying to be nice. Which is exactly why nothing is ever going to happen with Luke and me."

"Whatever, it's your funeral."

Suddenly a cell phone starts playing, but I don't recognize the ring tone. I look at Nicki. "Is that you?"

She shakes her head. "It sounds like it's *under* us."

We both jump up, and Fergus scrambles away. I lift a couch cushion and Nicki reaches for the phone. She looks at the call number and rolls her eyes again. "Speak of the devil—Ari's calling."

"That must be Luke's. *Don't* answer it; I don't want her to know he was here!"

Nicki waves a hand dismissively at me and flips open the phone. "Hello?" she says sweetly.

"What are you doing?" I whisper.

"This is Nicki, Luke left his phone at my house last night."

I stare at her bug-eyed.

"But if I see him before you do, I'll tell him you called, okay?" she chirps. "Later." She shuts the phone and laughs.

"What did you do *that* for?"

She shrugs. "Well, since you don't want to hurt her feelings, I figured it would be better if she thought Luke was at *my* house instead of yours. She already hates me, so what the hell?"

"*Or*, you could've just not answered it!"

"What fun would that have been?" She waves the phone

in front of me. "So it looks like you'll have to go to Luke's to return this."

I snatch it out of her hands. "Yeah, maybe, I guess."

She starts making kissing noises and I swat her on the arm. "Whether you like it or not, I *have* a boyfriend, so there won't be any kissing."

She narrows her eyes. "But you want to, you know you do."

I clench my jaw and sigh. "I'm going to my anniversary dinner tonight!"

"A restaurant is the perfect place to break up and avoid a scene."

"I'm not breaking up with him!"

Nicki shakes her head and looks at me like I'm an idiot. "Not five minutes ago you admitted he was up in arms about Samantha starting to see some guy—what does that tell you?"

"That maybe he was just looking out for Samantha? I can kind of see why he might be worried about her going out with a stranger from another country, and I'm thinking that isn't grounds to break up with him."

"Doesn't mean you have to stay with him either." She smiles and wiggles her eyebrows up and down. "Anyway, Luke is probably missing his phone by now. Why don't I get my car and I'll drive you over to his house." She smacks her lips.

I want to say no, but I also want to talk to Luke about what our next step will be. And yes, I also just want to see him. "Fine, but the only kissing I'll be doing today will be with Ryan!"

"Oh my God! That's great!" Luke gushes.

I climb the steps of the gazebo in his backyard, wishing my news *was* great. "Except the will says, 'irreversible condition with no *hope* for recovery,' and my mom hasn't given up *hope*, even if the doctors have. I'm pretty sure I can take the will to our lawyer, but if my mom doesn't change her mind, what do I do, take her to court?"

I lower myself onto the bench seat, and Luke looks at me with such sadness in his eyes. He sits down next to me and our legs touch. I catch my breath and shout *One-month anniversary* in my head. He holds out his hand and even though I know I shouldn't, I take it and he laces his fingers through mine.

Shivers.

"I talked to Nona about your mom."

"And?"

"Nona told her she's seen Remy before—she described her for your mom. She said your mom didn't seem too surprised."

I nod. "My mom confessed she thought she'd heard

Remy, and that a part of her has always known Remy was still around. But now that things are getting out in the open, why won't she take the next step?"

"Because she loves him," Luke says. "She just needs to realize that letting him go doesn't change that."

"What happened to your parents?" I ask, and immediately feel like I've overstepped my boundaries. I look at him and see his brow furrow. "I'm sorry, that's none of my business."

"It's okay. They died when Kayla and I were little—kayaking accident on the river."

That damn river. "I'm sorry."

"I don't remember a lot about them."

"I don't remember a lot about my dad either—just bits and pieces of things. I go and visit him all the time, but I've realized it's like visiting anyone at the nursing home—he's just another patient for me to bring Fergus to." I shake my head. "I can't believe I just said that, but I think it's true. Maybe that's why it's easier for me to imagine letting him go?" I bite my lip. "God, what's wrong with me?"

I turn to Luke to see if he'll think I'm a monster, but his eyes are soft and sympathetic. "Maybe seeing all of the other people in the home has given you perspective—you can tell the living from the dead."

"Maybe."

"Does your boyfriend know about Remy?"

His question catches me off guard. "I—I tried to tell him, but . . . no."

I breathe in the lilac-scented air. I feel the pressure of Luke's hand in mine, and I feel more confused than ever. "Ari called your phone this morning," I say, changing the subject. "Nicki answered it; she told Ari you left it at her house."

Luke groans. "I guess that's better than her knowing it was at yours."

"Why?"

"She apparently drove by my house that morning you came over and saw you. She said she asked you about it. I tried to be as vague as possible about the whole thing, because I didn't know what you told her, but it was obvious she was upset."

"I lied and told her I was here to ask Nona about my future with Ryan." Yes, think about a future with Ryan, I tell myself—instead of thinking about kissing Luke, who's lacing and unlacing his fingers with mine. I have absolutely no business sitting this close to him and holding his hand, but I can't make myself let go.

"Do you have a future with him?"

My stomach flips. "What do you mean?" I chance a sideways look at him and just about die seeing his dark blue eyes locked on mine.

"I mean, I'd kind of like it if you didn't."

"I don't know," I spit out as my heart pounds madly.

"Does he know you like I do?" he whispers.

He leans in and I feel his breath on my cheek. I turn to face him.

"And what do you know?" I whisper, my heart about to burst.

"Everything."

Our lips touch, and I feel like I'm floating. I know I should pull away, but God help me, I kiss him back instead.

ᑎᕦ FOURTEEN ᕤᑐ

I stand in front of the full-length mirror in my bedroom. Ryan will be here any minute. I turn in a circle and decide I'll keep the strapless blue dress on even if it's still a little too chilly for it.

Not that dressing up for Ryan makes up for the fact that Luke Amador kissed me earlier today—and that I kissed him back.

I scowl at my reflection. "You are a skanky ho."

I picture an announcer on one of those white-trash talk shows saying, *"Megan Sones is here today to tell her boyfriend she cheated on him with her psychic love toy."*

But it was just one kiss—one wonderful kiss—followed by many mentions of said boyfriend.

I plop down on my bed and wish I could be stronger, because liking two guys at the same time is just asking for an appearance on one of those shows, no doubt with Samantha and Ari waiting in the wings, ready to take me on in a bra-baring catfight.

I shake my head and try to concentrate on the fact that Ryan is taking me, not Samantha, to a swanky restaurant. Try to be happy and forget about the kiss.

I reach up and touch my lips.

That one electric kiss.

The doorbell rings, and Fergus barks.

"I'll get it," Mom calls out.

I rush over to my mirror again, looking for signs of guilt showing on my face. Remy appears beside me, her head hanging down.

"It's too late," she says sorrowfully.

"Yeah, you can't take back kisses," I reply, knowing full well Remy isn't talking about Luke.

She looks up at my reflections and smiles. "Blue dress." She pulls at the hem of her own dress and twirls around.

"Yeah. Love to stay and chat, but I've got a date and a lot of sucking up to do, because I was a bad girl today."

"She tried to use an apple," Remy says, pausing midtwirl and shaking her head, "but now they just use knives. I guess it works better that way." She reaches her hand toward mine, but I pull it out of her reach and jump back.

"Oh, no," I say, holding my hands up over my head. "We've already traveled this particular nightmare of a road before, and I really don't think I need to see any more dead girls or knives, okay?" I say, my voice cracking.

Remy nods. "Apples are nicer."

I stare at her bug-eyed as I back through my bedroom door. "Yeah, *apples*. Um, I'm gonna go now, okay?"

I run down the hall, and then look over my shoulder. I'm enormously relieved to see she hasn't followed me. I take a deep breath at the top of the stairs to compose myself, and then head down.

"Don't you look nice," Mom says quietly from the couch. I notice her eyes are red rimmed and she's looking worn-out. I assume she's been thinking about Dad and Remy, but I'm not getting any indication of which way she's leaning.

"Yeah, wow! Very nice," Ryan adds, looking me up and down. He's wearing a white button-down and a blue blazer, looking utterly adorable. My stomach flips nervously with guilt.

"Thanks," I say, feeling like a total creep. I turn to Mom. "Um, we'll be at the Ledges Dining Room at the White Mountain Hotel."

"The Ledges? Is this a special occasion?"

Ryan nods. "Yeah, it's our one-month anniversary today."

Why did I have to kiss Luke today of all days?

The phone rings and I rush to get it, glad for the interruption. I look at the caller ID and frown. "It's the nursing home."

Mom jumps up and holds her hand out to me. "I asked them to call me." She takes a deep breath and clicks the talk button. She listens for a few seconds with her lips pursed. "I see," she says. She covers the mouthpiece with her hand. "You two have fun." She waves us away and heads into the kitchen.

"Ready?" Ryan asks.

I look at Mom standing slumped in the kitchen and try to hear what she's saying, but then Remy floats down the stairs talking about apples again and I can't make anything out.

"Yeah, let's go."

Ryan looks up from his menu with a smile. "By the way, I got a bottle of champagne for later."

"How did you manage to get that?" I ask, hating how every nice thing he's done this evening is just making me feel more and more guilty.

First he gave me his jacket for the car ride because I didn't think to bring a sweater, then he opened the car door for me, held my hand in the parking lot, and pulled my chair out for me.

"Steven got it for us."

Steven—Samantha's brother. Why does everything circle back to her? Of course, Samantha's looking more and more like a saint compared to me. "So Steven doesn't mind contributing to the delinquency of minors?"

"Apparently not," he says with a sly smile. "My parents are out tonight, and I thought we could go back to my house and celebrate, if you know what I mean." He reaches across the table, takes my hand, and gives me a knowing look.

Oh, God. He's talking about doing *it*. I've been putting him off because I really wasn't sure I wanted to give it up to someone with—as Nicki put it—a groupie. My big excuse has been that we haven't been going out that long and it was too soon. Maybe he figures one month is long enough—no wonder he had the date memorized.

I force a smile on my face. "Hmmm, sounds intriguing," I murmur.

Our waitress, Marie, sidles up to the table and I could kiss her for preventing Ryan from making more detailed plans for later.

"Let me tell you about our specials. We have a roasted pork loin with apple chutney stuffing and garlic smashed potatoes."

I picture Remy babbling about the stupid apples and think I'll pass on that one.

"Pan-seared tuna covered with a wasabi-ginger sauce, a teriyaki vegetable medley, and spicy shrimp spring rolls. And finally we have a twin lobsters with crabmeat stuffing plate for two that comes with baked potatoes topped with sour cream and a side of steamers. Do you need a minute?"

"Yes, please," Ryan says.

Marie nods, looking weary. "I'll be back in a few."

Ryan licks his lips. "How about the lobster plate for two?"

I shake my head. "I think I'll just have the chicken piccata," I say, not wanting to get the "romantic" dinner for two.

"But I've heard lobster's an *aphrodisiac.*" He gives me a sultry look and I want to crawl under the table.

"I'm not a seafood lover," I lie.

"Really, you don't like lobster?" he asks, looking disappointed.

I shrug. "Sorry."

"That's okay, it's not like we *need* it anyway." He winks at me, and I know I have to break up with him.

"Ryan, I've been thinking—" My phone starts ringing and I fumble for my purse. "Shoot, I forgot to turn it off!" I grab it and see it's Nicki. She knows I'm out with Ryan, and despite the fact that she'd be cheering if she knew I was planning on breaking up with him, she wouldn't be calling unless it was an emergency.

"Let me take this out in the lobby. I'll, uh, be right back!"

I open my phone as I weave my way around the tables, earning annoyed looks from some of the diners.

"Nicki?"

"Hey, are you done having dinner with the rock star yet? I'm kind of in a jam."

"What's the matter?" I ask, glaring at an elderly couple that's staring at me.

"I stayed late after chorus practice talking to the assistant director, but when I got to my car, I couldn't find my keys. Everyone's gone, the place is locked up, and my parents are having a power dinner with one of my mom's clients, so I was hoping you and Ryan could pick me up."

"No problem! We haven't even ordered yet, but Nicki, I kissed him."

"Ryan? Big yawn."

"No! Luke! Actually, he kissed me, but I'm going crazy and I really, really need to talk to you about it."

She whoops into the phone.

"I haven't officially cut things off with Ryan so *don't say anything*, but—"

Nicki gasps.

"Are you okay?"

"Yeah," she says slowly. "I just thought I saw something at the edge of the woods surrounding the parking lot."

I hear breaking glass. "Nicki?"

"*Holy shit!* Something just smashed the light post by my car!"

"I'll get Ryan, we'll be right there."

"Megan," she says slowly, "there's definitely something moving in the woods—something big—and it's getting closer." Her voice is quaking. "Megan, I'm scared."

"What is it?"

I hear her phone hit the ground.

"*Oh my God, no! Leave me alone! Somebody help me! Help me!*" she screams.

My blood freezes as I realize this is what I heard when Remy held my hand during the blackout in the Haunted Forest ride.

"*Nicki?*" I scream. I hear shuffling noises and then nothing. "*Nicki, don't go in the woods! Don't go in the woods!*"

I hit the off button and dial 911 with shaking hands.

"911, what's your emergency?"

"My friend is at the North Conway Community Center and I think someone is after her!"

"After her?"

"She screamed and dropped her phone. Can you send someone over there right away?"

"I'll alert the police, please stay on the—"

I hang up, hardly able to breathe. I punch in Luke's number and pace up and down the hallway.

"Megan?"

"Luke, someone's after Nicki. She's at the community center, but I think—" I suck in a deep breath, not wanting to say what I have to. "I think the vision Remy showed me in that ride was about Nicki. I think someone's after her. I'm like ten minutes away and I'm scared I'm not gonna get there in time."

"I'm downtown with Ari—we can be there in a few minutes."

I shut my phone and run into the dining room. *"Ryan!"* I scream. *"We have to go right now!"*

We pull into the parking lot, and I see Luke and Ari talking to a couple of officers.

I rush out of the car and Luke points to me. "She placed the call."

"Did you find her?" I ask. I look all around the lot. Nicki's cell phone is on the ground near the driver's door of her car, surrounded by the broken glass from the lamppost. Her purse is a few feet away with her wallet and brush spilled out of it.

Ari shakes her head, worry filling her eyes. "There was no sign of her when we got here."

"Miss, can you tell me what happened?" a short, tubby officer asks.

"What happened is we have to look for her before it's too late!"

"Just hold on. We need a little information."

"There's no time." The officer isn't making a move to go after Nicki, and I shake my fists in frustration. "Okay, my friend Nicki called me like ten minutes ago and said she couldn't find her car keys. She thought she saw someone in the woods and then she said the light got shot out or something. She dropped her phone and I heard her scream." My lips tremble. *"She screamed for help."*

I look at Luke—he's the only one who understands what will happen if we don't get to Nicki in time. "We need to find her!"

He nods. "Officer, can we start looking for her now?"

The man shakes his head. "I told you before, this is a potential crime scene and I can't have you kids traipsing around destroying evidence. Bill," he says to the other cop, "call for backup, and tell Tony to bring the dogs." He turns to me. "Don't worry, Miss, we'll do everything we can to find your friend, and there's a good chance she got a lift with someone else."

I stare at him incredulously. "Oh my God! Look around. Why would she leave her stuff lying on the ground if she got a ride?"

Ari reaches out and squeezes my arm. "Don't worry, I know she's okay. I just know it."

"Let's not jump to any conclusions," tubby cop says to me. "I'm sure we'll find your friend safe and sound."

Ryan puts an arm around me, drawing me close to him. "He's right, Meg, let the police do their job."

"They're not doing their job; they're standing around while who knows what is happening to Nicki!"

I look out at the woods surrounding the back of the parking lot. Unfortunately, I know too well what might be happening to Nicki, and if I don't act quickly, Remy's vision will come true—if it hasn't already.

"You know what? If you're not going to look for her, I am!" I take off. Ryan snatches out for me, but I pull away. I race past Nicki's purse and ignore everyone calling after me.

"Hey!" the officer says. "Hey! Come back here!"

"Meg, no!"

I ignore them and keeping running, thankful I'm not wearing heels.

"I'm coming with you!" Luke says, catching up to me.

I turn around and see officer tubby holding Ryan back. "Meg!"

Luke and I crash through the brush and into the woods. *"Nicki! Nicki, where are you?"*

I weave around small saplings and bushes. Branches scratch my bare shoulders and legs. *"Nicki!"*

A small rock makes its way into one of my shoes. I

ignore the pain for a few seconds, then stop. "Shit! Shit! Shit!" I take off my shoe, dump the rock out, and frantically jam the shoe back on.

Luke stands at my side, breathing heavily. "Can you keep going?"

I nod and put my hands on my hips. *"Nicki?"* I scream as I look around, feeling the futility of this aimless search. "She could be anywhere." Tears pour down my face. I look around again, listening for any sound that might lead me to her. "We don't even know which direction she went in! We could be getting farther and farther away from her."

"Wait, Remy!" Luke says. "If she showed you the vision, she probably knows where Nicki is."

"Oh my God, yes! Maybe she can lead us right to her. *Remy!* We need you—we need you to help us find Nicki! Remy, can you hear me?"

"Remy!" Luke calls out.

Remy appears in front of us, shimmering softly in the darkness. In the faint light of the half moon I see her eyes are wide and staring. "Knives and apples," she whispers.

"Oh my God, Remy! Where's Nicki?" I ask, not wanting to think about knives. "Do you know where she is?"

Remy nods and turns around, walking silently over the dry leaves.

Luke takes my hand, squeezing it tight, and we head off

after her. Sirens wail in the distance. The cadaver dogs are arriving. I just pray we don't need them.

"Come on, Remy!" I say, feeling frustrated by her slow pace.

We follow her up a small hill. "Apples and knives. Bad apple. *Told you so*," she mutters.

"Nicki?" I call out for the hundredth time. Suddenly, I hear someone or something crashing through the brush just up ahead. *"Nicki?"*

"Hurry," Luke says, pulling me faster.

Prickers tear at my dress and cut my legs as Luke and I race past Remy toward the sound.

"Nicki, is that you?" I scream.

We round a boulder, and then I see her. *"No, no, no, no! We can't be too late."*

Luke wraps me in his arms and turns me away from Nicki's body sprawled out on the forest floor like a broken doll, her shirt cut open, revealing the hole in her chest where her heart used to be.

I cling to him as he hugs me tightly. "Oh, God, I'm so sorry. I'm so sorry," he says as he buries his face in my hair.

An icy chill envelops me. "This time knives," Remy whispers.

FIFTEEN

As Mom drives me past Nicki's house on the way home from the police station, I realize I'll never have another sleepover or movie marathon or anything with Nicki. And when Mr. and Mrs. Summers are done at the station, they're coming home to an empty house that will never be filled with Nicki's singing again.

I sink my face in my hands as fresh tears spill. I didn't think it was possible to feel this empty inside—or so soul-crushingly guilty.

Why did I assume that the second vision was from the past? And why didn't I let Remy take my hand when we were standing at the mirror earlier? Maybe she was going to show me that it was Nicki in the woods, and I could've gotten to the community center before practice let out—and she'd still be alive.

"Megan?"

I look over at Mom as she pulls the car into our driveway.

"We need to talk," she says as she takes the keys out of the ignition.

"Mom, I really just want to go in and lie down."

She breathes deeply, staring straight ahead. "I know the timing is bad, and I wish this could wait, but your . . . your father has pneumonia." She turns to me and purses her lips.

I nod numbly. I'd thought this might be coming when I'd heard him wheezing the day I'd brought Ryan to see him. While pneumonia can be potentially fatal for someone like Dad, he's recovered quickly in the past with antibiotics, and I'm not getting why Mom thinks I need to know this right now.

"I've talked with his doctors," she continues, "and they're going to let the pneumonia go untreated. He could—" Her voice cracks. "He could go any time," she whispers.

She bows her head and her shoulders shake. I'm speechless. If this is what I wanted, why do I feel like someone just punched me in the stomach?

"I just wish there was a way to be certain that he won't wake up—that I'm doing the right thing," she sobs.

I reach for her hand and she squeezes mine tightly. "I

think it is. No, I know it is. It's what he wanted," I tell her.

Even as I say the words, my stomach turns, because I can't help thinking that if Dad dies, I'll be responsible for the deaths of two people I loved dearly.

The doorbell rings and I raise my head off the couch pillow. I hope it isn't Ryan. I thought I made it pretty clear I wasn't up for any visitors, but he called after work, wanting to come by. I look at my watch—6:40. I roll my eyes. It has to be him. The bell chimes again. Mom's taking a nap and I know I need to get the door before he pushes the bell again.

"I'm coming," I mutter bitterly. I gently lift Fergus's head off my lap and shuffle to the door in my slippers. Seriously, what part of "my best friend was just brutally murdered and now I'm waiting for a call from the nursing home about my father's imminent death" does he not understand?

Of course, he still doesn't know I'm planning to break up with him, but in my defense I've been a bit too preoccupied the last few days to get the deed done.

I move in toward the newly installed peephole—after what happened, I bet we're not the only ones in town being extra careful—and my pulse races. It's Luke. I slide back the dead bolt and open the door.

"Hey," he says softly. "Are you up for a visit?" He runs his fingers nervously through his dark hair, and despite everything, a smile comes to my face. "I've been worried about you, did you get my messages?"

I sigh. I haven't returned any of his calls. If I did, I'd have to admit that what happened in the woods is my fault. I've lost too much already, and I've been afraid that if he knows the truth, I'll lose him too.

But he's here now, and even if he ends up hating me, I have to tell him.

"I wasn't feeling up to talking."

He nods and takes my hand in his. I feel my pain slipping from me. "No, don't!" I yank my hand from his. I won't let him make me feel better—I don't deserve it.

Tears gather in my eyes and I look away from him. He takes my chin and slowly turns my face back toward his. "Talk to me."

He leans in and our foreheads touch. I breathe in the mixture of paint and sweat on him.

"I'm here for you," he whispers as he takes my hand again. "I want to help."

I pull away and walk to the couch. "I could've saved her."

He sits next to me and I draw my hands up across my chest and rest my chin on them.

"You did everything you could."

"No, that's just it, I didn't. The night Nicki died, Remy tried to warn me. She reached out for my hand, but I wouldn't take it!" I look up at the ceiling as my eyes fill with tears for the millionth time in the last three days. "If I had just taken her hand, I might've seen Nicki, and she'd still be alive . . ."

"No! You don't know what you would've seen," he says. "It could've been anything. It takes an enormous amount of energy and concentration just for her to show up, let alone talk coherently. Even if she wants to show you something specific, there's no guarantee she could grab the image she wanted from the correct time frame."

Luke reaches out again, and this time I let him take my hand. I lean my head on his shoulder, and he kisses the top of my head. "There's nothing you could've done to stop this."

The phone rings and my eyes fly open. I jump up and pick it up from the charger. My heart drops when I see it's the nursing home. I push the talk button, say a quick "Hello?" and hold my breath while I listen.

"Okay, I'll let her know. We'll be right there." I hang up and bite my lip.

"Is it time?" Luke asks.

I nod.

"Get your mom. I'll drive."

I cling to Luke as Mom kisses Dad on his freshly shaved cheek. "I've never stopped loving you," she whispers.

The machines that usually flash and beep next to him

have all been disconnected and turned off, making his jagged and labored breathing seem overly loud in the quiet room.

My heart races as I watch his chest fall with each exhalation, wondering if it will rise again. His face is ashen, and the skin across his closed eyes looks thin and papery.

A part of me wants to erase the last week and go back to the way things were. But seeing him so small and frail in his bed—his body eroded away from years of disuse—I remind myself that this is what Dad wanted *ten years ago*.

Mom takes one of Dad's hands and sits in the chair next to his bed. "Is . . . is she here?" she asks, looking around the room. Her eyes are wide and frightened, but I know what she wants. She wants to see Remy—to see her before she finally moves on.

Remy's nowhere in sight, and I turn to Luke. He shakes his head. I'm not sure if we should call her. Tonight Remy should move on with Dad, but what if she starts ranting beforehand? The last thing Mom needs is to witness one of Remy's tantrums.

Mom stands up, kisses Dad's hand, and lays it gently on his chest. "Can you get her here?" she asks Luke, desperation in her eyes. *"Can I say good-bye to my baby?"* she cries.

Her lower lip quivers, and Luke nods.

"Do you think we should?" I whisper, hoping Luke will

remember Remy's fit the day Nicki saw her. I don't think Mom could handle it if Remy has one of her episodes.

"I think it'll be okay," he says to me. "This is what Remy's been waiting for."

He holds his hand out to Mom. Tears stream down her face as she takes it. "Remy, it's time," he calls out quietly. "Remy."

We all look around the room. I see Remy forming in the far corner and exchange a look with Luke. He points in Remy's direction and Mom shakes her head.

"Remy, Mommy's here," I say. "She wants to see you."

Remy comes into view more clearly and Mom gasps. "Baby?"

Remy starts to skip in a tight circle. "Star light, star bright, first star I see tonight. I wish I may, I wish I might, have the wish I wish tonight."

Mom's face crumples and she covers her mouth with a hand. "Baby, I'm sorry, I'm so, so sorry," she whispers.

Remy turns and her eyes lock onto Mom's. *"Mommy?"* She solidifies and beams at Mom. "Where have you been? Have you seen Daddy? I need to find him! Bad apples!"

Mom holds out her free arm and Remy rushes to her. Mom sucks in a deep breath, no doubt chilled to the bone now that Remy's laced her arms around her waist.

"Megan," Luke whispers, pointing to my father.

I turn and watch him exhale a jagged breath, and then lie completely still. A soft glow surrounds him, getting brighter by the second.

"Mom!"

"I, uh, see it," she stutters. "Remy, honey, *go with Daddy. He's here. Go with Daddy!*"

The glow rises and I see my father's face muted and distorted in its midst.

Remy pulls away from Mom and cocks her head toward the light. "Daddy? Daddy!" she squeals. "I've been looking for you everywhere!"

Relief rushes through me. It's almost over. Dad and Remy will finally be at peace.

The light starts to fade and Remy looks wildly around the room. "Daddy? Daddy, where are you?"

Oh, no! Why didn't she go with him? Her face screws up in anger and I know she's about to lose it. "Luke!" I call out, hoping he'll know enough to break his link with Mom.

I hold my breath for a second until he drops Mom's hand. Mom looks around the room and I know she can't see or hear Remy anymore. Thank God!

"Daddy, I thought you were gonna help me! Daddy? Daddy?"

Mom turns to me, and despite the fact that I want to curl into a ball and scream, I put on my poker face.

"Did—did she go with him?" she asks.

Remy's calling over and over for Dad, and all I can think is that I need to get Mom out of the room quickly before Remy blows something up.

"Yes," I lie. "She went with him. She's at peace now." I embrace Mom and start to lead her out of the room. "We'd better alert the doctor."

She pauses and looks back at Dad with such pain in her eyes. Dr. Macardo told me at our last session that in cases like this, the family has often already mourned their loss years before the actual death occurs. Mom's red-rimmed eyes and blotchy face say otherwise, and I can't imagine how she'd feel if she knew that Remy was still here.

We flag down a nurse, who nods at us sympathetically. "I'll get the doctor right away. I'm sorry for your loss."

Remy's starting to quiet down, and it sinks in that she'll probably be with me for the rest of my life.

⌒ SIXTEEN ⌒

Ryan will be here any minute now. I've barely had the strength to get up in the mornings, let alone break up with him, but I know I can't put it off any longer.

Two days ago, the White Mountain Chorus sang "For Good" from *Wicked* as Nicki's casket was lowered into the ground. Ryan draped his arm around my shoulder. I looked at Luke standing in the crowd next to Ari and saw the hurt in his eyes. It felt so wrong pretending it was Ryan I wanted comforting me. It felt so wrong seeing Ari clinging to Luke.

I'm *so* tired of pretending and living a lie. At least this is one thing I have some control over, no matter how hard it's going to be.

I remember how horrible I felt after Jason broke up with me sophomore year. He said he needed space, but I knew it was because I wouldn't sleep with him. Nicki told me I was better off without him because being dumped for not putting out is all kinds of wrong. But my ego was bruised for months.

I even considered sleeping with him just to get him back—and so the hollow feeling I had in my stomach would go away. Luckily, Nicki's constant reminders of her feminist manifesto kept me from going through with my stupid plan. I just wish she were here to know I'm finally doing the right thing and excising myself from this love triangle. And once I quit Land of Enchantment, I won't have to worry about Ari.

Thinking about Ari makes me feel even guiltier. She's been calling to try and cheer me up and convince me I need that spa date she booked more than ever. I feel bad, because if it wasn't for Luke, I think Ari and I could've been friends.

Unless you're one of those girls who blows off her friends for a guy, I remember Ari saying.

I sigh. Not only am I blowing her off for a guy, I'm doing it for the guy she's in love with.

The doorbell rings and I steel myself. At least Ryan has an afternoon shift at the park to get to, so hopefully this won't be a long, drawn-out mess.

I check the peephole and pull back the bolt. "Hey, thanks for coming over."

"I'm glad you were finally feeling up to a visit," he says. "Even if it's a quick one." He leans in to kiss me and I turn my head so it lands on my cheek.

"Here, let's sit down." I lead him over to the couch and he takes my hand. God, I feel like such a creep. "So how are things at the park? Has Samantha been promoted yet?"

He shakes his head in disgust. "I haven't talked to her much lately, she's too busy with *Christophe*. But I heard some of the exchange students talking at lunch yesterday, and apparently the two of them got *caught* in the dorm rooms—if you know what I mean. Everyone's talking about it."

"Caught as in . . . ?"

"As in caught in bed."

"Oh my God!" I say, thinking that in a million years I never would've predicted that, but maybe after saving herself for Ryan all these years she couldn't control herself.

"Yeah," Ryan says. "I mean, what the hell was she thinking?"

"Uh, maybe she was thinking she has a boyfriend?" I cringe inside as soon as the words leave my mouth. That was probably not the best thing to say to my soon-to-be ex who *I* refused to sleep with. Of course, having lost two very important people within days of each other has probably not had the best effect on my sensitivity chip.

Ryan raises his eyebrows and I sense things are heading south fast.

"Well, I guess," he says, looking at me like he's caught on to where this conversation's going, "that some people don't *mind* rushing into things."

My first thought is, *Touché*, but then I remember why Ryan and I never did the deed.

"Or maybe some people don't want to rush into things because they can't shake the feeling that their boyfriend really wants to be with his best friend. And you know what? From your reaction to Samantha and Christophe being caught with their *pants down*, I'm thinking I was right all along."

Ryan clenches his jaw. "Look, I know things have been pretty tough for you lately, and I've tried to be there for you, but it's obvious you're not ready to let me in yet. I totally understand, but maybe this isn't the best time to talk and I should go." He stands up and heads for the door. "I'll call you in a few days."

"Ryan, I don't think we should be together anymore."

His shoulders slump and he lets out a long breath. "Let's talk about this in a few days, okay?" he says, still facing the door. "When you're feeling better."

"This isn't something I just thought of on a whim," I say

quietly. "It's actually something I decided last week."

He turns to me, looking puzzled. "Last week *when?*"

I hang my head. "When we went out to dinner—well, kind of *during* dinner."

"Oh, that's great. What were you gonna do, dump me after dessert or after we'd gone back to my house and toasted our anniversary?" he asks bitterly.

"Honestly, I'd only gotten as far as thinking how truly awful the timing was."

"Really? Why, because I'd planned a romantic evening for you? Or was it just too much for you to handle that *Samantha's* brother bought the champagne? God, Meg! How many times do I have to tell you there's nothing between Samantha and me?"

"Look, you can say that all you want, but there is something between you. This isn't just because of Samantha; it's mostly because . . . because there's someone else." I feel my face flush and wish I could fast-forward time, have him storm out of my house, and have this awful feeling in the pit of my stomach go away.

"Someone else, as in you're seeing someone else—now?"

"Kind of. It's not like I was sneaking around, well, not on purpose—and it's not like anything big happened."

His mouth drops open in surprise. "Okay, so you give me all kinds of shit about Samantha, who I never *once* made a move on no matter how many openings I had, and you go ahead and cheat on *me*?" He shakes his head. "Wow, I thought I knew you better than that."

"That's just it: You don't."

"I guess you're right about that, 'cause I never saw this coming." He cocks his head at me. "It's that guy at the park, the one who came looking for you in the ride, isn't it?"

I bite my lower lip and nod. "I didn't want to hurt you," I say, my voice trembling as tears stream down my face. "It just happened. So much has happened and the last thing I wanted to do was hurt you."

"You know what?" he says softly. "You're right. A lot's happened and you've got more to deal with right now than any person should have to. I just wish I was the one you wanted to help you get through it. Good-bye, Meg."

I let him leave, and as he shuts the door, I pull my legs to my chest and hug them close, letting my tears soak into my jeans. I think it almost would've been better if he'd left with screams and angry accusations echoing in my ears, instead of reminding me what a great guy he is, making the fact I've hurt him cut even deeper.

A chill fills the space around me and I turn to see Remy sitting next to me, staring ahead and chewing on the end of one of her braids.

God, help me.

I shake my head. It's only a matter of time before Remy makes her presence in the house known to Mom—just when Mom and I were starting to reconnect. What will happen when Mom realizes I lied to her?

Remy takes the tip of her braid out of her mouth and looks at me with fierce determination on her face. "She d-doesn't mean to be," she spits out finally. "She can't help it. But she's really, really bad. *Make a wish.*"

She starts to shimmer out of focus, and I reach out for her, only to have my hand pass through her icy body. "Wait, who?"

"Bad apple," she whispers as she disappears.

I clunk my head down hard on my knees. "I can't go through my life like this," I whisper. "Why didn't you go with Dad?"

I get up and pace back and forth.

What did Nona say? That Remy was scared and she was looking for something.

She was looking for Dad. That was a no-brainer—she'd only asked where he was a gazillion times. But what if Dad wasn't the only thing keeping her here. What if the thing she's scared of is what prevented her from going *with* Dad?

She obviously knew what was going to happen to Nicki, and that certainly qualifies as scary to the hundredth degree.

I sure as hell hope there isn't something worse than that coming down the road!

And the apples—what do the *freaking* apples have to do with anything? And why does she keep asking me to make a wish?

My head is spinning trying to process all of this.

"Why won't you go away?" I scream.

I breathe hard, waiting for Remy to appear, but she doesn't even pop up to give me a disjointed babble about bad apples.

I desperately need help—and not the Dr. Macardo kind.

I walk through the kitchen and scribble a quick note for Mom. I grab my house key from my purse and throw it in my backpack on my way to the garage.

I open my phone and push Luke's contact number, thankful he's got the day off from work.

"Hey, it's me. We need to call out the big guns. We need Nona to walk Remy into the light or wherever the hell she needs to go—today!"

I brush my sweaty bangs aside as I wheel my bike up to Luke's porch. He offered to come get me, but I wanted more time to think. Not that it did me any good.

All I think is that someone was killed at the Land of Enchantment site hundreds of years ago and a similar murder has happened again. But how could two girls get killed the same way? And who's to say the first murder was even at Land of Enchantment?

The only explanation is a ghost, but do ghosts kill? You'd think that kind of thing would be in the news—yeah, maybe not. And I'm certainly no expert on the supernatural. Maybe ghosts can kill.

I go to press the bell, but the door flies open. Nona is there, shaking her head and looking sorrowful. She reaches out and places her pudgy hands on my cheeks. "I send blessings to you, and thanks that you and your mother are becoming a family again."

My first thought is to ask how we can be a family now that Dad's gone, but then I understand. Now we can move on after being on hold for ten years—we can heal.

Except that Remy's still a factor.

I see Luke standing behind Nona and feel an overwhelming longing to rush into his arms, but Nona clucks her tongue and shakes her head. "No time for that," she says as if reading my mind. "This way." She points down the hall to a room I haven't been in before.

Luke runs his fingers across my shoulder as I pass. I catch my breath, and he follows me silently into the room. It's obvious Nona wants to get right down to business.

A round table sits in the middle of the room draped in a

red velvet cloth. Matching curtains are pulled shut, making the dimly lit room even darker. Three candles—one yellow, one white, and one orange—have been placed on the table in front of three chairs.

"Okay," Nona says to me, "you go here in front of the white candle. Luka—"

"I know," he says, pulling out the chair in front of the orange candle.

Nona nods appreciatively. "Good boy! You've been paying attention. Maybe I'll pass the business to you when I retire in ten years or so."

Despite everything, I can't help smiling at this seventy-nine-year-old woman talking about retiring sometime in the next decade.

She takes a bunch of dried herbs tied tightly together and lights it on fire. After a few seconds she blows out the flame and walks around to each corner of the room waving the smoldering stick up and down.

"She's smudging the room—it's a kind of supernatural cleaning," Luke says. "The sage will cleanse the room of negative energy and lavender is for a calming effect."

"I hope she used extra lavender," I whisper, thinking we'll need a double dose for Remy.

Once she passes all four corners of the room, she rubs the stick on a metal plate to snuff it out. "Now," she continues, "let's join together as we state our intentions for today."

She sits in the empty chair in front of the yellow candle and slides her hands across the tablecloth toward us. I follow her lead and reach out for Luke's hand, while Nona takes my other one.

Luke's hand makes me feel warm and safe, while Nona's cool, tight grip practically buzzes with electricity.

Nona looks up at the ceiling, which I notice for the first time is painted with the constellations. It reminds me of the ceiling of Grand Central Station in New York City, which I visited with Nicki. A tear stings my eye and I try to shake off the memory. I need to have a clear head for this. Luke gives my hand a squeeze as if he knows I need a boost, and I give him a thankful smile.

Nona taps the table in front of me impatiently, and I focus back on her.

"Thank you, universe, for giving me the gift to help this young lady," she calls out loudly. "Thank you for allowing me to help her sister move on to your next realm, so that she may join her father and find the peace that waits for her."

She bows her head and I do the same.

Next, she reaches into her housecoat and pulls out a pack of matches. She strikes the match and lights her candle.

"The heat of the candle attracts the spirits. Yellow is for persuasion and protection."

It's obvious why she's chosen that candle; she'll need it to help persuade Remy to move on.

She gives the matches to Luke, who lights his own candle.

"Orange for attraction and encouragement—this one will help bring Remy here and encourage her to listen to us."

Luke passes the pack to me. I strike the match and move the flame to the wick.

"White for purity, and truth," Nona says.

"So we know why she's still here," I say.

"Yes," Nona says, "there'll be no cryptic answers today. I will open the way between our world and Remy's, and she will speak to us without the interference of the time streams. We will get the truth from her."

I watch my candle flicker and burn, and then Nona clears her throat again.

"Did you bring something of Remy's?"

"Yeah." Luke told me to bring something that Remy might like. I'd searched our room—now mostly devoid of our old things—until I had remembered the necklace.

It was just a twenty-five-cent plastic heart I'd gotten in a vending machine at the grocery store. Remy loved to wear it, and whenever I protested that it was mine, she just laughed and said that if I loved her, I'd let her wear it—and I did. Remy always got her way.

I reach into my purse for the necklace and give it to Nona. She examines it briefly, and then places it in the center of the table.

"Remy, we ask that you join us here," Nona says with authority.

Remy appears by my side, with her arms folded across her chest. "Who are you?" she asks grumpily.

Nona scoffs. "You've been to my house before, little girl, you know me."

Remy shakes her head and starts to turn away, but Nona holds her candle out.

"Feel its warmth, Remy, come to me to warm yourself. See what your sister brought for you."

Remy faces Nona again, scowling. The temperature in the room drops dramatically and my heart starts to pound. This isn't going as smoothly as I'd thought it would.

Nona holds up the necklace with her other hand and smiles. "Would you like this Remy? If you tell us why you're here, I'll let you have it."

The necklace flies from Nona's hand and lands in the fireplace. The logs ignite and the pink plastic heart melts from the chain.

I stare at Luke, and his wide eyes tell me he's just as

surprised as I am that Remy's getting the upper hand so quickly. Perhaps Nona's experience hasn't prepared her for a seven-year-old with a temper.

Nona puts her candle down and calmly pushes up her sleeves with a look of determination on her face. "*Remy!* Tell me why you're here. Why didn't you go with your father?"

The room grows colder still. My body starts to shiver, and I lean closer to my candle to gather whatever feeble heat I can from it.

"Daddy was gonna help, but he left me! *He left me!*" She stamps her foot and I jump as a wave of river water splashes up over the table, extinguishing all the candles.

My teeth are chattering as the cold water seeps into my T-shirt. Shit! If Remy's conjuring up water from the river, things are about to blow.

Nona stands up, glaring at my sister, who matches her stare with the look of a defiant little kid determined to get her way.

"It is time you went into the light. Your father is waiting for you," Nona says. She stands and holds her hands up above her head, chanting under her breath. A bright glow the size of a fist starts to form over the table. It grows as Nona rocks back and forth muttering, "Help this tortured soul find her way to your peace, help this tortured soul find her way to your peace."

"No! I won't let her hurt you, Meggy!" Remy screams. *"Daddy where are you?"* she wails. Remy disappears and reappears in different places around the room. "Daddy?"

"He's there," Nona yells, pointing at the light. *"Go to him!"*

Remy reappears next to Luke and stares at Nona with hate in her eyes. *"No! You're not my mother, you can't tell me what to do,"* she says through gritted teeth.

I didn't think it was possible to feel any colder, but an icy wind starts to whip around the room. Droplets of water fly off Remy and form snowflakes in the air that drift to the carpet. Frost forms on the tablecloth and my eyes grow wide as the candles freeze and crack apart.

I want to help Nona, but it feels like the cold has frozen me in place, and I can only watch the scene, praying Nona can get things back in control.

Luckily, Luke jumps up and rushes to Nona's side just in time to catch her as she collapses. "Nona!"

The room grows slightly warmer as my sister sneers and disappears.

Luke helps Nona sit back in her chair. "Are you okay?"

Nona mutters some sort of blessing and then looks across the table at me. Her face is pale, and sweat has gathered on her brow. "She's filled with *such* rage." She takes some tissues from her dress and mops her face. "We'll begin again. Luka, we need new candles."

"No!" Luke and I cry out in unison.

"You're going to rest now!" Luke commands.

Nona sighs and nods her head wearily. "Maybe you're right, we should try again when I feel stronger."

Luke helps Nona up and leads her out of the room with an arm around her waist.

I realize I'm shaking uncontrollably, and it's getting harder to breathe. I fumble through my purse with numb fingers and find my inhaler. Trembling, I raise it to my lips and take in as deep a breath as I can manage. I exhale as Luke rushes to me.

"Your lips are blue!" he says, wrapping his arms around me. "I need to get you warm. Let's go up to my room."

He leads me out, very much like he did with Nona, and helps me up the stairs to a small room under the eaves of the house. The walls are covered with paintings, and my heart sings when I see myself looking out from a watercolor picture on an easel by the window. He's painted such a joyful expression on my face, and I can't help wondering when was the last time I felt like the girl in his painting—if I'll ever feel that way again.

He pulls aside the sheets and the down comforter, and I sit on the bed. I hesitate for a second, and then lift my wet shirt up over my head and slide my feet under the covers—too cold for any modesty. He takes his own shirt off, gets in the other side, and nestles in next to me, pulling the blankets up past our shoulders.

His skin burns against mine, and I try to take in the heat so I can stop shaking. He holds me tight, rubs my back, and kisses my hair. Soon my trembling stops, and I concentrate on the pounding of his heart. I look up at his blue eyes so full of concern, and tilt my chin to kiss him.

He kisses me back gently, but I want more. I want to forget all the pain. I want to forget Remy. I want to feel alive again. I kiss him hungrily, and he pulls back.

"Megan?"

"Shh," I whisper, as I pepper his bare chest with kisses. I run my hands up his strong arms and then kiss him on the mouth again. I press my hips into his, and then reach around to unhook my bra and slide the straps down off my shoulders. I hug him tightly and bury my head in his neck. "Whatever happens—just don't stop."

ᕲ SEVENTEEN ᕲ

ow," I say as Mom pulls the car into the Land
of Enchantment parking lot. "I can't believe how
many cars are here." It's packed and it looks like
more people are arriving to take advantage of the late-day
ticket price. If you arrive after five, you only have two hours
until the park closes, but you can use your ticket for another
full day anytime during the summer.

Of course, none of this matters to me. I'm only here
because Mr. Roy called to let me know I had a paycheck
waiting for me. It's just one day's pay, but I'll get it, and then
let them know I won't be returning.

In a few minutes, Ryan, Samantha, and Ari will be part
of my past, and I can concentrate on my future with Luke.

A smile comes to my face and my heart flutters thinking about being with Luke last night—the one good thing among the seemingly endless nightmares that have happened.

Except, with Remy haunting me, how many more nightmares am I going to have to suffer through? My good mood fades as quickly as it came. If Nona couldn't get through to Remy, who can?

"Here we are," Mom says, pulling up to the office building.

"Thanks, I'll get the check and be out in a few minutes."

I open the front door and make my way to Mr. Roy's office, praying I don't run into Ari. I can imagine her taking one look at my face and knowing I was with Luke.

I breathe a sigh of relief when I reach the door, and knock.

"Come in," Mr. Roy calls out.

I open the door and Mr. Roy smiles at me sympathetically. "How're you doing, Megan?" he asks.

"Um, okay, I guess."

His eyes glisten and I hope he's not going to cry. "I want you to know how very, very sorry we were to hear about your losses."

I nod. "Thanks, and thank you for the flowers you sent."

He dabs the corners of his eyes with his pink hankie and motions for me to sit down.

"Um, my mom is waiting for me, I really can't stay."

"Actually, I was hoping you could. I'm in a bit of a pickle, you see. We have a group of kids visiting from the Shining Star Camp today. Do you know it?"

"Yeah, it's for kids who are terminally ill," I say. "Our school does a fund raiser every year for them."

He smiles again, his eyes misty. "We let them come to the park free of charge, and I'm sure you understand how much it would break my heart to have any one of them disappointed with their visit."

"Uh-huh," I say, trying to figure out where he's going with this.

"Well, when I had lunch with the group earlier today, there was a little girl, four years old, dark hair like yours, and I asked her what would make her visit to Land of Enchantment special. And do you know what she said?"

I shake my head.

"She wanted to meet Snow White." He looks at me expectantly.

"Oh," is all I can think to say. He's still giving me a puppy-dog face, and I really just want to get out of there.

He folds his hands on his desk, looking utterly pitiful. "Unfortunately, the Snow White on our schedule for today, Sarah Goldstein, came down with a stomach bug. I was really hoping I could talk you into filling in for her."

Oh, God. The last thing I want to do is get *that* outfit on and walk around the park. And what if I run into Ryan—or Ari? "Uh, I'm sorry, but I'm not really feeling up for that, Mr. Roy. I was actually going to tell you I won't be coming back to work here this summer."

He looks wounded and tears up again.

"You know, with what happened and all," I say quickly. "Can't someone else do it?"

He shakes his head and dabs his eyes. "As soon as little Lucy told me about her wish, I got right on the phone and tried to find a replacement. We're shorthanded today, and I can't pull anyone off of a ride—safety rules, you see. Do you think you could find it in your heart to work for just a couple of hours until the park closes? For Lucy's sake?"

I look into his watery eyes and don't know what to say.

"What if I just take you to Lucy and then you can go? I'd credit you for a full day's pay—that's how much it means to me to make this little girl happy."

He looks like he's about to bawl and I nod my head. "I'll call my mom," I say wearily.

I walk into the costume room and my heart pounds. It's quiet, but my eyes dart around the room, waiting for Remy to pop up. I reach out to grab a size eight Snow White costume and brace myself, afraid of getting another vision. I exhale as nothing happens, and I take the costume off the rack without incident.

Why did I let Mr. Roy talk me into this? And why does a man his age have to be such a freaking crybaby? Of course it would take someone like him to run Land of Enchantment—who else would be into all this drivel?

I walk into the changing room, take my clothes off, and slip the costume over my head. I lace up the bodice and I can't help thinking about the girl Remy showed me—and about Nicki. I bite my lip. After Luke took me home last night, my first thought was to call Nicki.

I hear the costume shop door open and some people giggling. I take a deep breath and put on my "everything is A-OK" face.

I walk out of the dressing room and jump. Samantha and Christophe are going at it like Ye Olde Costume Shoppe is a cheap hotel room. Her shirt is pushed up, her bra is unhooked, and Christophe is helping himself to her boobs as he presses her up against the closed door, blocking my escape.

I squeeze my eyes shut and turn my back to them, adding the image of Samantha being felt up to the collection of scary images in my head. I clear my throat. "Hey, uh, sorry to be a party crasher guys, but I kinda have to get to work."

"Oh my God!" Samantha squeals.

"Can I turn around now?" I ask after hearing them shuffling around for a few seconds.

"*Oui.*"

I turn and see they're both red faced.

"*Megan!*" Samantha squeals. "I'm so sorry, we thought everyone who was dressing up was already out in the park so the room would be empty for a while."

Christophe shrugs. "It is our break time," he says in his thick accent.

I nod like all the employees are hooking up on their breaks. "Well, I'm gonna get going, but might I suggest you finish your *break* in one of the dressing rooms? You know, in case someone else might need to come in here."

I walk past them into the hall, and Samantha follows me out. "Hey, Megan, are you doing okay?" she asks shyly.

I nod and put on my smile.

"If you need anything, you know you can call me," she says, straightening her shirt. "And sorry about before with Christophe—it's just hard to find places to be alone."

"No problem."

She looks up at me and purses her lips. "Ryan told me that you broke up with him."

"Yeah. He's all yours now."

"What do you mean?"

"I mean, it wasn't a secret you liked him."

"Oh." She looks down at her shoes for a second and then back up at me. "Are you really over him?"

"Yeah, I'm actually seeing someone else."

Her jaw drops. "Seriously?"

"Yeah, it was kind of unexpected."

She smiles slyly. "Well, since you're seeing someone else, I guess I can tell you. Ryan came over to my house after you dumped him and finally made a move—but I turned him down." She looks giddy. "I'm having fun with Christophe, and you know what? I'm kind of glad it's Ryan who has to suffer in silence for once."

"And maybe *he'll* make the soul mate confession at the next keg party."

Her face flushes deeper. "He told you about that?"

"Yup."

"I was really drunk, I never would've told him otherwise. Not that I should've said it in the first place, but . . ."

"It's okay. Honestly, I could never shake the feeling that you were right."

"Maybe." She furrows her brow and twirls one of her braids. "If you ever want some company when you visit the nursing home again, I'd be happy to go." Her eyes suddenly grow wide. "I mean, if you still were planning on going, but maybe after your dad, um, maybe you're not."

"No, I'm still planning on going, I just don't know when."

"Okay, whenever you're ready, you can call me. I really did like going there, except for that Mr. Archulata. He kept rubbing my thigh and it kind of freaked me out."

"Yeah, he's a little too friendly." Talking about Mr. Archulata reminds me of Nicki, and it's getting to be a strain maintaining "the face." "Um, I should get going. Mr. Roy is waiting for me."

Samantha looks at her watch. "I have to get back to work soon too. Don't forget to call me."

"Sure." Even though the senior citizens eat up her perky shtick as if it were tapioca pudding, I'm thinking I'll let Samantha Lee Darling make her own arrangements to visit the home. It'd be too weird for us to go together with her being friends with Ryan.

She reaches out and gives me a quick hug. "You can call me if you just need to talk too."

I nod, plaster a smile on my face, and make my way out to the park to meet Lucy.

Mr. Roy is waiting for me in a golf cart outside the office building. He clutches his hands to his chest and beams. "I just know Lucy will be thrilled to meet you, Snow White." He winks and I will myself to keep my happy face on.

I'm really not sure I'm up for this, but I also don't want

to disappoint some little kid. What would Samantha do if she were playing Snow White?

I hold the skirt out and curtsy.

Mr. Roy smiles and pats the empty seat next to him. "The group from Shining Star is at the Fun Farm visiting the animals. I'll bring you over."

As we drive slowly through the park, I see that the crowd tonight is definitely mostly older kids—all the really little ones must've had enough hours ago. As it is, it's obvious families are calling it a day and are making their way to the exit in droves.

A few people point at me as we drive by. Because of the extra money Mr. Roy is paying me, I smile and wave and do my best Snow White.

He pulls up near a group of kids in bright blue Shining Star Camp shirts. They're gathered around an Asian woman dressed as Mother Goose, and I wonder how Henrietta Stupin's broken hip is.

"Everyone," Mr. Roy says as he parks the cart. "Look who I found roaming in the Haunted Forest."

One little girl with dark hair runs to me. "Snow White!" she says. "Mr. Roy said you'd come."

"Hi, Lucy," I say.

She gapes at me. "How'd you know my name?"

I look at Lucy and take in the circles under her eyes.

Be Snow White, I think, *channel Samantha.* "A little birdie told me."

She smiles widely. "Do you want to see the bunnies?"

I nod and take Lucy's hand, the back of which is sporting a yellowish brown bruise just like my Dad's used to from where the nurses inserted IVs.

I bite my lip. Keep it together, Megan!

I walk her over to the rabbit pen and kneel down.

"That white one with the pink eyes is my favorite," Lucy says.

"He's a special fellow," a familiar voice says.

I look up and see Miss Patty.

"Are you having fun, Lucy?" she asks.

Lucy nods and runs back to join her group. "Mr. Roy told me you're leaving us," Patty says quietly as I stand up. "Are you sure we can't convince you to stay?" She points to Lucy, who is hopping around like a rabbit.

"I really just need some time to myself," I say.

"I understand, and maybe it's for the best. But if you ever do change your mind, we'll always have a place for you."

"I'll keep that in mind," I say politely.

Suddenly a whistle pierces the air. "Yo! Snow White!"

A man is walking my way with four sunburned kids and a harried-looking wife in tow. "Group photo!" he barks.

It's obvious he's spent too much time in the Brothers

Grimm Tavern, but Miss Patty waves me toward him. "Go on," she whispers.

I put on my happy smile and bend down toward one of the kids. "I'm Snow White."

"So?" she asks sullenly.

The father pulls me toward him, and I try to maintain my smile despite wanting to choke on his beer breath.

"Max! Get in the picture."

Max rolls his eyes and scowls at me. "This is so *stupid*! Can't we just go back to the hotel and swim?"

I want to tell Max I think that's a very good idea, but his dad swats him on the back of the head and then corners a woman walking by and demands she take the picture.

He puts his arm around my waist as his wife herds the kids toward us. "Smile," she says, even though it looks like her toddler is about to lose it.

I feel the man's hand sliding down my waist toward my butt and I jump out of his arm, determined not to add being groped to my list of problems. "You know, I think I should stand with Max!"

Max looks horrified, but I put my arm around him and beam for the camera. "Say 'Land of Enchantment!'"

The family mumbles, "Land of Enchantment," and I wave to them as I walk off.

"Have an enchanted evening!" I look at my watch. The

park closes in thirty minutes. I only agreed to stay long enough to meet Lucy, but Mom went home to rehearse with Fergus until I call her to pick me up. She's got a competition to practice for and I know how much she hates it when I interrupt her.

I poke my head around until I see the Shining Star group. I guess I can hang out with them until closing—it's certainly safer than being dragged into another photo op.

Only thirty minutes and I'm done with Land of Enchantment forever!

∽ EIGHTEEN ∽

The park loudspeakers start playing the closing lullaby, and I realize Mr. Roy must've recorded Ari singing it. It's really pretty, but I can't help thinking Nicki would've sounded better—her voice had a strength and clarity that Ari's doesn't.

I turn away from Lucy and my shoulders slump. I drop my smile, feeling utterly exhausted from trying to maintain the happy face, and fight back tears. It's amazing how many little things make me think of Nicki. I still can't believe she's gone.

"Good-bye, Lucy, it was very nice meeting you today," I say, not looking her in the eye.

She hugs me. "Good-bye! Thanks for playing with me!"

"My pleasure," I call out as the group heads toward the exit.

When the song ends, Mr. Roy's pre-recorded goodbye message plays for the departing crowd.

"On behalf of our entire Land of Enchantment family, I want to thank you for spending your day with us. May you have a safe journey home. We hope to see you again soon."

"You won't be seeing me again," I whisper as I make my way to the office building to change out of my costume.

"Hey, Megan!"

Casey Winters is running down the path. She stops in front of me, panting. "Miss Patty wants to see you."

"Oh, I forgot to get my paycheck."

"Are you going to the party at Dillon's house?"

I shake my head. "Not feeling much like partying."

"Oh yeah, sorry," she says, avoiding eye contact. "Um, if you change your mind, though, stop by."

She rushes off and I sigh. I can't wait to be alone with Luke tonight.

I head into the office building and wind my way through the halls toward Miss Patty's. I round a corner and freeze.

I hear Nicki singing.

"My cage has many rooms, damask and dark. Nothing there sings, not even my lark."

My heart pounds as I slowly approach the office, certain

I'll see Nicki's ghost waiting for me there. I'm not sure if this is a good or bad thing, but if she's there, maybe she can tell me what happened to her.

"Nicki?" I whisper as I walk through the door, only to find Ari facing the mirror.

She sings another line as she lightly runs the fingers of one hand up and down the gilded frame. *"If I cannot fly, let me sing."*

I stare at her, my blood pounding in my ears. "You sound just like . . ."

She turns to me and gives me a cold smile. "Like Nicki? Do you think they'll finally give me a solo *now*? I mean, it's not an exact copy of her voice, but it's *pretty damn close.*"

"What . . ." is all I can manage, not comprehending what she just said.

"First, why don't you shut the door," she says sweetly, but there's venom in her eyes, and the hair on the back of my neck rises.

Adrenaline pumps through me, and I start backing out of the room. "I think I should go," I choke out.

Ari rolls her eyes. "Yeah, no," she says calmly. She opens a drawer in Miss Patty's desk, pulls out a small gun, and points it at my head. *"Shut the door."*

I gape at her. "Is this a joke?"

"No, the joke is I thought you were my friend." She

waves the gun toward the door. "Now, are you going to close the damn thing already?"

Not taking my eyes off Ari, I reach back, feel the knob, and push the door shut. "Why are you doing this?"

"Because a little birdie showed me this." She moves to the right, and I have a clear view of the mirror.

"Oh, God," I whisper as Luke and I appear in the glass— in his bed. I stare at the scene playing like a movie. "H-how did you . . ." I squeeze my eyes shut. "Make it stop!"

"That's enough, Mirror. I've witnessed that particular betrayal more times than I can stomach anyway."

When I look up, the room is reflected in the glass again.

Ari narrows her eyes.

"I'm so sorry, I never wanted to hurt you," I say.

"I'm so sure. You were pretty smart, though. Having Nicki answer Luke's phone was genius, I never thought to keep tabs on you," she says. "When the mirror showed me Nicki and Luke in his car, I thought *she* was making a move on him, but it was you all along." Ari shrugs. "Oh, well, at least I got the voice out of the whole messy deal. Who knows? Maybe I'll be Broadway bound after all."

"*You* killed Nicki?"

"No, but we have a little tradition in my family. Do you know the story of Snow White?"

I stare at Ari incredulously. "*What* are you talking about?"

"I'm talking about my ancestors. Way back when, Snow White married her prince, only there wasn't a happily ever after. Seems the prince was a bit of a dog and couldn't keep his hands off the servants and she saw it all, courtesy of my little friend here." She points the gun to the mirror, and the face appears.

It bows its head to me, staring at me with its dark, smoky eyes and a smirk on its lips. If I didn't know any better I'd think it was enjoying this.

"You said it was just animatronics . . ."

"Yeah, I lied about that. This here is a one-hundred-percent-certified magic mirror—it shows me anything I want."

"This isn't happening," I say, hoping I'm going to wake up.

"As I was saying," Ari continues, "poor Snow White sought comfort with the only man she could trust—the one who spared her life." Ari looks at me expectantly. "Care to take a guess?"

I shake my head.

"Party pooper! It was the woodsman. He fell in love with Snow White the moment he set eyes on her. When her stepmother ordered him to cut Snow White's heart out, he couldn't do it, and he let her go."

Bile rises in my throat as I realize what this means. "*You* cut out Nicki's heart!"

Ari takes a deep breath and points the gun at me again. "I'm *trying* to tell a story here. Don't you want to hear the stuff that isn't in the books?"

"Ari, no, please just let me go." Tears come to my eyes as I think about what she did to Nicki, and how I set this all into motion.

Ari waves the gun in a circle. "Sorry, but the person with the firearm gets to makes the rules. And right now you have to listen. Better yet, watch. I've seen it a hundred times. It's really quite riveting, kind of like the History Channel and a horror movie all wrapped up in one. Mirror, would you be so kind?"

The smoky face smiles broadly for a second, and then disappears as if a wind had come up and blown it apart. I see the girl from the vision Remy showed me in the costume room.

"*Ari, no,*" I beg, already knowing just how badly this story ends.

The girl—Snow White—is crying and trying to pull away from a broad, rough-looking man who is holding her firmly in his arms. "What?" she says. "Take Eliza from the only father she's ever known to run off and live in the *woods*, are you mad?"

"Eliza is *my* daughter!"

"It doesn't matter. I'm the queen now, for God's sake! I can't just walk away from everything."

He tries to kiss her, but she turns her head away from him.

He grabs her tighter and shakes her. "I alone have been faithful to you, yet I still have to share you with that pig!"

She pushes against the man's chest and breaks loose but falls as she tries to run. He's on her in a flash and pins her arms back above her head. "Eliza is mine; *you are mine!*"

She struggles and kicks at him. "No. I told you from the start I could never leave him."

Rage boils on his face. He reaches toward his leg with one hand and draws a knife strapped to his calf. "I will not share you," he says coldly.

I turn my head as she screams.

"Stop it!" I cry out. *"Please!"*

"He finally made good on her stepmother's orders—too bad the old queen didn't live to see it," Ari says.

I stare at Ari, who just returns my look with a faint smile. "You're crazy. This is all crazy. It can't be true."

Even as the words leave my mouth, I know I'm wrong, because my sister has already shown me the end of this particular fairy tale. And now I know why Remy was going on and on about apples and knives: The queen tried to kill Snow White with the poison apple, but it was the hunter's knife that finally did the trick. A trick the Roys have apparently adopted.

"Remy!" I whisper. I need Remy!

The door opens behind me and I jump.

"What's going on?" Miss Patty asks. She looks back and forth between Ari and me. "*Arianna Roy!* Put the gun down!"

"Don't you have something better to do right now, *Patty*," Ari snarls.

Patty looks behind her shoulder, and then shuts the door. "Don't worry, Megan, everything will be okay."

Relief floods through me until I see Ari's face twisted with rage, and I get the feeling she's too far gone to listen to anything Patty has to say.

"Everything's not going to be okay, *Mommy*. She knows what happened to Nicki, and if she tells, you're going to get in a lot of trouble."

Patty's mouth drops open. "Me? I've only ever tried to keep you away from that damn mirror!" She runs over to it. "I knew this was going to happen! I knew it! What did you show her?"

Luke and I appear on the surface again and Patty gasps. "Oh, for God's sake! Stop!" she shrieks at the mirror. "Why do you torment her like that? You know what she does afterward, but that's what you want, isn't it? More blood."

The face resurfaces and its hands appear folded under its long, pointy chin. "I merely do as I am commanded—it seems young Arianna is the one with the taste for blood."

Patty turns to Ari and holds out a hand to her. "Don't listen to that thing! Come on, honey, it's too late for you and Luke, you know that. Why bring her into this at all?" she asks, tilting her head toward me. "You know what the mirror's like, it's just trying to goad you into doing something you don't want to do."

"Oh, I want to do it, and this time it'll work!" Ari hisses. She walks around the desk toward me and I step back until I bump up against the wall. She points the barrel of the gun at my heart, and my legs shake. "This is what Luke wants," she says, tapping the gun on my chest, "and if I can get it, he'll be mine."

"It's too late for that," Patty says shrilly. "Tell her!" she yells at the mirror.

The face cocks his head, eyeing Ari and me. "I've told her as much many times," it says. "I warned you, Arianna. I warned you that Kayla's heart would not get you what you desired, but you wouldn't listen. Having consumed it, you'll never be more than a sister to him now."

"You killed Kayla?" I whisper. *"You killed Luke's sister and ate her heart?"*

"Shut up!" she shrieks. She turns to the mirror, all the while keeping the gun pointed at me. "Hers will *counteract* Kayla's heart. I know it will, and Luke will love me as much as he loves her." Tears flow down her cheeks. *"He just has to!"*

"It might work," the mirror states matter-of-factly. "If he loves this girl enough, it might work."

I shake my head in disbelief. "You can't be serious. This is insane!"

Patty looks at me sympathetically and then turns back to Ari. "There are other boys, honey."

Ari scowls at her stepmother. "You just don't want me to be happy."

Patty's eyes open wide with surprise. "How can you say that? I was the one who begged you not to do anything to Kayla. I told you it wouldn't work!"

"You knew?" I ask, stunned.

Patty turns to me with a shocked expression on her face. "Oh, I . . ."

"Yes, Miss High and Mighty knew," Ari says smugly. "Why don't you tell Megan which ride Kayla's buried under? And how you delayed the installation of the new ride so we could stash Nicki's body there before the cement base got poured. Of course, we weren't able to get her body here since *someone* was poking around in the woods with my boyfriend!"

I stare at them in disbelief. "How could you?"

Tears pull Miss Patty's makeup down her face in streaks. "You don't know what it's like living here with this thing badgering me all the time. And Arianna always gets her way. Always!"

Patty faces the mirror. "I *begged* you not to show Ari anything. I begged you and now . . ." She turns to me. "And now I guess we really don't have a choice. I'm so sorry, Megan. I tried to warn you."

I didn't think it was possible for my heart to pound any faster, but realizing Miss Patty is throwing me to the wolves sends it into overdrive. "Oh my God, you're not going to let Ari do this? You can't. If you let me go, I won't tell anyone. I promise."

Ari smiles smugly. "This is a done deal, we just need to wait for—"

"Remy!" I scream. *"Remy, I need you!"*

"Yell all you want," Ari says. "The park is closed, there's no one here."

"Remy!"

The mirror laughs. "This should be quite interesting."

"What are you talking about?" Ari barks.

Remy appears before me, and the room grows colder. "Told you so."

"Oh my God, Remy! You knew all the time, didn't you? You knew the mirror was real, and you knew what they were going to do. That's why you didn't go with Daddy."

"Bad girl!"

"Who the hell are you talking to?" Ari asks, looking bewildered.

"Her sister," the mirror answers.

Ari scoffs. "She doesn't have a sister."

"I wish I may, I wish I might," Remy rambles.

Blood is pounding in my ears and I feel like I've gone totally insane. "You know what I wish? *I wish to God I wasn't in this room right now!*"

"Done!" the mirror calls out.

Suddenly the floor feels like it's shifting beneath my feet, and in a flash I'm in the hall. "What?"

I hear Ari and Patty yelling from inside the office.

Mr. Roy is standing in front of me and he jumps in surprise.

"Mr. Roy!" I shriek, not caring why I'm in the hall, just grateful I'm not trapped with those lunatics on the other side of the door. "You have to help me! It's Ari, she killed Nicki and Kayla, she has a gun, and she was going to kill me too!"

Mr. Roy shakes his head. "My little princess never killed anyone. That's what her daddy's for." He slowly raises a long silver hunting knife and tips the point toward my chest.

"I'm very disappointed in *you*, Megan. I didn't think *you* were that kind of girl. I could've had any number of girls work in your place today, but after Ari told me what you did, well, I was in full agreement that it was time you joined your good friend Nicki. Feisty little thing, she was."

I back away. "This isn't happening. Mr. Roy, please tell me this isn't happening. Ari's got a gun . . ."

"The gun was just to keep you in the room until I got there. Ari's a delicate thing. She has no interest in the hunt— she just likes to reap the benefits."

"No," I whisper. "Not you." My head is spinning. How could Mr. Roy—

A gunshot goes off in Miss Patty's office, and then Remy appears by my side.

"Meggy, run!"

And I do.

◦◦ NINETEEN ◦◦

I bolt down the hall and hit the doors to the park. I burst through and keep running. The light is fading, making it easier to hide—I hope.

I run past the Mermaid Lagoon and hear Mr. Roy calling my name.

I turn left and see Hansel and Gretel's Haunted Forest. Without thinking, I sprint toward it, scramble over the locked gate, and run inside the employee entrance. I don't stop until I get to the witch's kitchen.

I wildly look around for a hiding spot. We were warned it was downright dangerous to ever get off the safety paths, but I think that in this situation it would be way more dangerous to be out in the open. I scramble over the safety barrier and carefully pick my way across the track, past Hansel in his cage, and crouch down behind the Gretel robot.

My heart pounds and it's getting harder and harder to draw a breath. Of course my inhaler is in the costume shop—with my cell phone. I will myself to take deep calming breaths. "Remy?" I whisper. "Remy, I need you."

"Shh," she whispers back, appearing shimmering and happy. "You made a wish," she says in a hushed voice. She claps her hands quietly.

"Is that how I got out of the room? Because I made a wish?"

"Star light, star bright, first star—"

"Okay, I get it," I whisper back. But how did my wish get me out of the room? Ghosts don't grant wishes, but . . . but . . . genies do! What if genies can inhabit things other than lamps? Like mirrors.

But why didn't Ari just wish Luke would love her? Unless she doesn't know what the thing in the mirror is! I shake my head. Obviously she doesn't; if she did, my night with Luke never would've happened.

"I wish I was home!" I blurt out.

I brace myself, but nothing happens. I rest my head on my knees. I must need to be with the mirror for it to grant my wish. Crap!

Oh, no. That damn mirror can also show the Roys

where I am if they ask it! But will they, or are they already out in the park looking for me? If the gunshot I heard hit someone—most likely Patty—I'll have Ari and Mr. Roy to deal with, and that scares the hell out of me!

I might not have much time. I hug my knees tighter. I need help. "Remy," I whisper, "get Luke! Tell him I'm in trouble. Tell him to come right away!"

Remy nods. "Nice boy."

"Go tell him where I am, tell him I need help! Go!"

She disappears and I try to make my body as small as possible, hoping Luke finds me before Mr. Roy does.

I hear Mr. Roy calling my name and my blood freezes. He's getting closer. I don't know why he's bothering to call me, like I'd answer him, but I guess maybe he's hoping to flush me out like a bird in a bush.

I huddle back against the wall.

"Megan? Where are you?"

Oh my God, that's Luke.

"Megan, I'm coming!"

I suddenly realize Mr. Roy can simply follow Luke right to me! And what if Mr. Roy decides to kill Luke too? *I am such an idiot!*

"Remy!" I say as loudly as I dare. "Remy, tell Luke to go away. *Please!*"

"Megan, I'm coming," he calls out, sounding like he's right in front of the ride.

"Remy! Do something!"

"Mr. Roy?" Luke sounds surprised, and then there's silence.

Oh, no!

I stand up just as the ride comes to life. Hansel starts rattling in his cage and an empty car enters the witch's house. I need to wait for it to go down the slope into the oven section before I dare jump back over the track.

"Hurry up!" I yell at the car. I need to see if Luke's okay. Tears stream down my face. He's got to be okay!

The car stops in front of me, and Gretel slides out to push the witch into the oven. The wall lifts and the car drops out of site. I'm about to jump across when I see Remy by the control panel and Mr. Roy coming up right behind her. With Gretel out of the way, I'm completely exposed.

"Bleeding," Remy mutters.

I glare at Mr. Roy. "What did you do to Luke?"

"I never wanted a hunting dog before," Mr. Roy says, eyeing me from across the track. "I usually like to hunt my quarry myself, but with so much ground to cover, Luke arriving when he did was especially helpful. But his usefulness is over now."

"What did you do to him?" I scream.

"Let's just say he's out of commission for now. But if we make this quick, I can get him the attention he needs. I wouldn't want to disappoint my little girl, after all."

Another car enters and the witch cackles madly. *"Into the oven!"*

The car careens around the room and comes to a stop. Gretel slides out again, and part of me just wants to tell him to get it over with, but I can't leave Luke.

"Now, let's see," Mr. Roy says as Gretel slides back toward me. He taps a finger gently on the tip of the knife and surveys the area I'm standing in. "There's really no place for you to go. That should make my job easier." I see him tense up, ready to jump the barrier and cross the track.

"Into the oven," the witch shrieks as another car enters.

Blood is pounding in my ears.

"Bleeding. Bad apples."

The car stops in front of me, Gretel moves toward it, and Mr. Roy leaps across the track. My heart races as I scramble across the metal bar Gretel slides on, holding my arms out for balance, and trying not to fall before I can reach the car.

"No!" I shout as the oven door rises and the car dives down the incline before I can get there.

The strobe lights in the oven flash and I jump down onto the track, hoping I can run into the oven section before the wall comes down.

I feel Mr. Roy grab the ribbon on the back of my costume and the knife slices into my shoulder. "Ah!" I gasp as I feel blood seeping into my costume, and then the pain seers through me.

"Almost done," he pants in my ear. He starts to wrap his arm around my neck, but I jab my elbow into his stomach. He cries out and I turn to face him as he doubles over. I push him as hard as I can, hoping to send him down the track into the oven.

The witch knocks into him as she goes back to her starting place, and he falls flat on the track. He starts to pull himself up, but the oven door slams down across his middle. Blood gushes from his mouth onto the track, and I scream again.

"Bleeding," Remy says.

Another car enters and I scurry off the track to the control panel, breathing hard.

"Into the oven!"

I stare at Mr. Roy's lifeless body for a few seconds and then hit the emergency stop button. The car heading toward the oven stops and I bolt toward the exit. I have to find Luke.

Luke is lying on the path a few feet from the exit of the ride. I rush to him and kneel down. His chest moves, and I cry with relief. His shirt is soaked with blood, though. With trembling hands I gently pull his T-shirt up to see if I can stop the bleeding.

I gasp when I see the deep wound on the side of his abdomen. Blood rushes from the gash and I know Luke won't make it if we have to wait for an ambulance. "I love you," I whisper and then I dash off toward the office building, knowing I need to make another wish.

I race into Miss Patty's office and stop short when I see Ari sitting in the chair with her feet up on the desk. Oh, God, why isn't she out in the park?

She sits upright in surprise. "Well, isn't this convenient," she says as she picks up the gun. "I'll tell Daddy he can stop looking for you. All the stupid mirror could show us was you crouching in the dark somewhere." She cocks her head. "Although, from the looks of that cut on your shoulder, it appears Daddy found you after all. You must be quick, he doesn't usually let anyone get away."

She picks up her cell phone and starts to punch in some numbers.

I touch the blood dripping down and realize my arm is throbbing. "I wish Luke's wound was totally healed," I blurt out.

The mirror flashes behind Ari, and she spins around in the chair. "What's going on? What are you doing?" she asks the mirror.

The face appears and looks at me with one eyebrow

raised. "Nicely played," it purrs, "but you've let the cat out of the bag now."

Ari pushes the chair away from the desk and looks back and forth between the mirror and me. Her eyes widen, and she puts her phone down. "That's how you disappeared from the room—you *wished* it!" Her eyes grow even bigger. "How many do I get?" she asks the mirror.

The face purses its lips, as if trying to delay answering her. It lets out a tired sigh. "Three. Everyone gets three."

Ari turns to me with an evil glint in her eye. "Three! Can I wish for anything I want?"

"I cannot take or restore life, and it is also beyond my powers to alter love. But as you know, there are other ways to get around that particular limitation. I do think you should see what's become of your father before you proceed any further."

The face disappears and Mr. Roy's battered body appears, with the oven door above it, smeared with his blood.

Ari puts a hand to her mouth and gasps. "Daddy!"

The face fills the mirror again, and it bows its head. "You could save your stepmother's life, though, there's still time."

Ari turns and I follow her stare. Miss Patty is sprawled out on the carpet, blood leaking from a small wound in her stomach. Patty moans and Ari shakes her head and scoffs. "The hell with her, but Daddy, I wish Daddy was okay!"

The mirror smiles coldly. "I'm afraid I cannot grant that wish, but your stepmother . . ."

Tears gather in Ari's eyes. "*No!* I'm not wasting a wish on her! She can rot in hell for all I care."

I look at Miss Patty and I'm torn between doing the right thing and saving my last wish. I shake my head. There've been too many deaths already. "I *wish* Miss Patty would fully recover from her injuries after a stay in the hospital," I say, making sure she'll be okay without adding her to the madness already in play.

The mirror looks at me with surprise and then flashes. Patty coughs from the floor and Ari laughs crazily. "You just wasted your last wish! Are you insane?"

I nod. "Yeah, I think I am."

"I win!" she says with glee in her eyes. "I finally win! All the suffering I've been through will finally be over." She turns to me and shakes her head. "The only downside to all this is that you won't be around to see what you've lost—to ache for what you can't have."

She stares at me coldly, and then her eyes light up, making chills run up my spine. She walks over to me and twirls the gun on her fingers. "I can't wish Luke was in love with me, right?" she asks over her shoulder to the mirror.

"Correct," it says.

She taps my chest with the barrel of the gun. "And

cutting out hearts is messy. But could you use your magic to *switch* our hearts?"

"Yes!" The mirror's smoky eyes burn with admiration. "Yes! Very clever, Miss Arianna!"

Ari beams as she looks me up and down. "Looks like you're going to lose your heart after all, but at least you'll still be alive."

My hands fly to my chest as I stare at Ari. "No," I whisper. God! Why did I throw away my last wish?

Ari nods. "I mean what *fun* would it be if you didn't live every day knowing Luke was making love to *me* instead of *you*?" She purses her lips. "And there'll be nothing you can do, because who would believe you? It's perfect!"

Oh my God. She's going to do it. My mind races. I don't have any wishes left and Ari has a gun—my options are extremely limited.

"She's a bad apple," Remy whispers.

Remy! If I can get her riled up, maybe she can destroy the mirror, or at least keep Ari from making a wish until I figure something out.

"*Remy*, that bad girl is gonna make some wishes that will hurt me. Do you hear me, Remy? I need you to stop her!"

Remy appears in front of Ari. Ari shivers, obviously feeling the cold air.

"*Bad apple!*" Remy growls. "Leave Meggy alone!" A blast

of wet, frigid air swirls around the room, whipping my hair around my face. "No more *wishes!*"

"What's happening?" Ari calls out, her eyes looking wildly around the room.

I smile at her. "Arianna Roy, I'd like you to meet my sister, Remy."

Remy solidifies and I hear the roar of the river echo around the room. My breath frosts in the air as the cold increases.

"Really bad apple!" Remy says.

"Arianna, hurry! Make the wish!" the mirror calls. "Quickly!"

"I wish—"Ari starts to say, but Remy stamps her foot and a wall of water swirls around Ari.

Remy looks at Ari with hate in her eyes. *"I said no!"*

The water engulfs Ari, forcing its way into her mouth and nose. Her hands flies to her throat as her eyes bulge.

"Remy, stop!" I scream as I realize Ari is drowning. I make my way toward the water and force my arm through the freezing whirlpool. Ari reaches out one hand, but as our fingers touch, I realize I can't save her—I won't. Nothing can save Arianna Roy from herself, and no one is safe if she lives.

I pull my arm back, and my body shakes as the room grows even colder. Large snowflakes fly around, and the whirlpool freezes into a frothy wall of slush until Ari is finally encased in solid ice.

"I'm sorry," I whisper, looking at Ari's wide frozen eyes staring out blankly. One clawed hand is still clutched at her throat. I wouldn't have wished for this ending in a million years.

Remy smiles. "No more bad apples."

"Remy . . ." I don't know what to say to her. I didn't mean for Ari to die, but at the same time, I can't say that I'm sorry either.

Remy plops herself down onto the rug at the base of the ice wall. "Meggy, where's Daddy?" she asks wearily.

I walk over to my sister and kneel down. I smooth out my bloodstained skirt and hold out my hand. Remy slides her chilly hand into mine.

I catch my breath as shivers wrack my body. I wait for some awful vision to hit me, but there's nothing—just Remy and me sitting on the floor like we're getting ready for a tea party.

"Daddy's waiting for you," I say. "You just have to look for the light. He's there, and Nicki too—they're waiting."

A glow surrounds Remy, and she rubs her eyes with her fists. "I'm tired, Meggy."

"Go to Daddy and you'll feel better."

The glow gets brighter, and for half a second I wish Remy would stay.

"Are you gonna . . ." Remy trails off, turning her head toward the growing light.

This is it—this is the last time I'll be with my sister. "I'm gonna be fine, Remy," I choke out.

Remy stands up and brushes her wet bangs back, squinting into the light.

"Remy," a voice calls out.

"Daddy?"

"I love you, Remy," I sob as the light engulfs her.

She looks back at me. "I love you too, Meggy."

Remy fades from view, and the room warms. The ice starts to drip and then turns to water, dumping Ari's lifeless body to the floor.

It's over now. It's finally over. I pick up the desk phone to dial 911.

Before I dial the numbers, I look up at the mirror. The face is gone, but I'm sure it can see me anyway.

"Are you happy now, you miserable hunk of glass? Is this what you wanted?" I say, pointing to Ari's body. My lip curls up in disgust. "Just you wait. I know someone who'll be more than happy to make three wishes for me, and believe me, you'll be sorry you screwed with my life."

❧ TWENTY ❧

Luke and I duck under the police tape and he runs the flashlight across Miss Patty's office until he zeros in on the mirror.

It's been two weeks since I was last here. I wanted to get back sooner, but Luke thought we should wait until things cooled down to lessen the chance of running into the police.

We stand on the other side of the tape, and Luke puts a hand on my shoulder, giving me strength.

"Are you up for this?" he asks.

I nod. With Miss Patty's confession, the excavators have already dismantled six rides and recovered the bodies she knew about, including Kayla's. There's no telling how many more bodies they'll find that were buried before she met Mr. Roy.

Luke and I researched missing persons from the area, and there have been at least a dozen over the years—including Mr. Roy's older sister, who co-owned the park until she vanished, or as the article we read states, "ran off to Europe." And I'd bet money someone's remains are stashed under Hansel and Gretel's Haunted Forest.

"Let's do it," I say. We walk slowly up to the mirror. I stare at our reflection illuminated by the flashlight and can't help thinking that Nicki and Kayla would still be alive if it weren't for the thing inside. I know the genie wasn't responsible for the actual killings, but from what I've seen, it certainly encouraged them. And if it's as old as I think it is, it's no doubt been causing misery and murder for centuries.

"I'm back," I say to the mirror.

The face appears, and Luke jumps. "Whoa," he whispers as he takes my hand.

I'd warned Luke about it, but in the darkness of the room, its glowing eyes and smoky face look more chilling than ever.

Its lips turn up in a hungry smile. "Ah, company. How delightful. I've found it very tedious hanging here with no one to talk to. Time moves so slowly when there's nothing to occupy the mind."

I scoff. "I'm sure the police would've loved to have chatted with you!"

The genie arches one of its dark eyebrows. "Actually the police did prove to be entertaining for a bit. Their theories about Miss Arianna's death were quite amusing."

Luke and I exchange looks.

The coroner determined that Ari had drowned, but he was unable to figure out how it happened on dry land. The CSI team identified river water in her lungs, and Patty—God bless her—stuck to the story that she didn't know how things transpired, but that I came in *after* the fact. Arianna Roy's murder will no doubt have them puzzled for years.

"Yeah, so glad Ari's death provided you with some fun," I say. "Anyway, it's time you found a new abode, but first we have a few questions."

The mirror smiles, and goose bumps break out on my arms. "Answering questions is my specialty."

"Why are there two of you? I reread 'Snow White,' and there should be only one mirror."

Its smile fades; it's obviously disappointed by such a mundane query. "Mr. Roy's great-grandmother liked to consult with me often, and thought it would be easier if there was one in the park and one in her home. She wished it to be so."

I scowl. "Oh, I'll bet you just *loved* having an extra opportunity to mess with her head."

"I am only here to serve," it insists.

"We can get rid of that when we, you know . . ." Luke says to me.

I nod.

"Is there anything else you'd like to divine?" the mirror asks politely. "I can show you people you might be curious about."

"No, I think we're good," Luke says.

"Wait," I say as a question pops up in my mind. "I am actually curious about something. Can you show me who Samantha Lee Darling's soul mate is?"

"Oh, but you might not like the answer," the mirror says, though there is a glint in its eyes that tells me this is what it does best—playing with people's emotions.

"I think I can handle it."

Ryan appears on the surface of the glass and I smile.

"This pleases you?" the mirror asks, its face reappearing, the sparkle in its eyes replaced by a look of confusion.

"Yes, actually, it does."

Luke gives me a look. "Are you ready *now*?"

"Um . . ." I say as my thoughts race. Despite what I know about the mirror, the fact that it can show me *any-thing* makes me wonder if we shouldn't be so quick to carry out our plan. I could see Mom—see what she's really thinking when she's alone. See if she really meant what she said about becoming a family, about wanting to be part of my life again. And Luke? There are a million questions I could ask about Luke.

I look up and see the mirror's eyes boring into mine and catch my breath. This is what it does: It offers you glimpses of your world that you weren't meant to see, and then it destroys you with them.

I swallow hard. "Yeah, I'm ready."

Luke clears his throat. "We did some research, and without a handy lava pit to chuck you into, we don't have the power to destroy you—at least not the original you."

"And we don't think it's safe to let you influence anyone else either," I continue. "So we got Miss Patty to agree to donate you to the nursing home where my father lived."

The mirror raises its eyebrows, and I smile. "But we'll have to take away your power first."

The mirror scoffs. "I was placed in this mirror by the strongest of magics, and nothing can diminish my powers."

"Well, we're not really taking away your power," I say. "We're just going to prevent you from *using* it."

I squeeze Luke's hand and he nods. "I *wish* that you can no longer show your face or communicate with another person until the end of time," Luke says.

The mirror's mouth drops open. "No, wai—" The surface flashes with light, and then our reflections reappear.

"One down, two to go," I say.

"I *wish* the second mirror you created was destroyed."

The light flashes again.

"And finally, I *wish* that you are unable to fulfill any wishes inadvertently made in your presence."

The glass flashes once more, and I know it's over—finally, finally over. Luke turns the flashlight off and takes me in his arms. I hear his heart beating, and feel safe at last.

Since Ari and Mr. Roy died, I've read all of the Brothers Grimm fairy tales. I've tried to guess which ones might be true and which ones might still be unfolding after all this time. But as I read those stories filled with beasts, magic, and murder, I saw that there was always the side trip through hell that came before the happy ending. I think I can safely say I've lived that hell, and it's time for my happily ever after.

I tilt my chin up and kiss Luke.

"I love you," he whispers.

"I love you too." I lay my head back on his chest and think that one of these days I'll be smiling like the girl in the painting in his room.

SINK YOUR TEETH INTO
ANOTHER NOVEL BY AMANDA MARRONE:

UNINVITED

I close my eyes, hoping he won't come tonight. It's later than usual. I hope he's given up, or just gone, and I can finally sleep. Cool air blows through the window, and I marvel at my bravery. Or stupidity. It's opened just a crack, no more than an inch. But until tonight I've kept it closed, so I know he'll be wondering what it means.

I listen for some movement in the branches outside, but the leaves are dry and noisy now. I open my eyes—I have to look. It's better when I see him coming. I put every ounce of energy into listening, waiting for my eyes to adjust to the dark. I turn my head, grimacing at the sound of my long hair against the pillowcase. I look out my window, searching the branches, wondering if he'd still come if I chopped down the tree.

"Jordan, are you awake?"

My heart races as I hunt for Michael among the branches. His dark form is pressed against the trunk a few feet higher from his usual perch. How long has he been watching me? He drops down, settling in closer to the window, and I remind myself to look for an ax in the morning.

"Jordan, let me in."

"Go away, Michael. I will never let you in." My voice is steady and calm, without emotion. I've said these words a hundred times today, so they'd become automatic. So I wouldn't change my mind.

Michael sighs, and I think I see him nodding. He knows I'm not ready to let him in. I suspect he knows I think about it, though. I suspect he knows that a part of me wants to.

"You don't know how good you have it, Jo."

I don't like where this is leading. This won't be a "let's talk about the future" night. Michael's missing his old life and he'll keep me up for hours if I encourage him.

"Did you go to school today? Did anyone talk about me?"

I roll my eyes. "This is high school, Michael, you're old news. People have found better things to gossip about. I mean, dying in the summer . . . well, your timing was way off. If having people remember you is important, that is. There's just way too much happening, people move on pretty quickly.

Now, if you had died during the school year, that would have made a bigger impact."

"God, Jo! This isn't easy for me, you know."

I nod and wonder if his eyes see better than mine. Can he see I'm putting on an act, that every inch of my skin tingles when he sits outside my window? "I'm sorry, Michael, but I'm tired. I need to sleep."

"But I miss you, Jo. It's not like you think. I can't sleep. I can't sleep at all. I'm awake with nothing to do. Nothing to do but think, and miss you."

"I'll leave some books outside for you tomorrow. Maybe you can accomplish something you never did when you were alive—you can actually read a book. Or, hey, how about this? You can walk into the sunlight and end this all. Have you thought of that? What would happen if you walked into the sun?"

Michael's quiet, and I think he may keep it short tonight—until he taps his foot on my window.

"How's Steve and Eric?" he asks. "They still playing ball?"

"Oh God." I turn my back to the window. "Ask me something I care about. Your stupid friends are exactly the same as they were when you were alive. They live and breathe football or basketball or whatever stupid ball season it is. They still hang out with their gorgeous girlfriends and they still smash mailboxes after a few too many beers. I'm surprised you haven't joined them. That was one of your favorite pastimes, wasn't it?"

He doesn't answer, and I remember Michael making out with some girl—one hand up her short skirt, pressing her against the lockers—acting like he wasn't making an ass of himself. I wonder how many guys walking past dreamed of trading places with Michael? I know how often I dreamed of trading places with that girl.

"So, what, they don't talk about me? Like, not at all?"

He's definitely not letting it go tonight. I think he actually thought they'd worship him forever.

I turn back to the window, but I remember to move slowly this time. I've seen my cat throw itself against the window trying to catch the birds outside in the tree. I sometimes wonder if Michael will lose patience with me and begin to think of me like that, like a bird. Like his prey. So I move bit by bit because I don't know what I would do if Michael were to throw himself against the glass.

"I lied before," I finally say. "Everyone talks about you. They actually talk about you a lot." I pause and let Michael think what he will. "But they're not reminiscing. They think you killed yourself." I've wanted to tell Michael this for a long time, but he was such a mess over the summer, it didn't seem right. But tonight I'm feeling mean, and I won't baby him. Besides, he doesn't seem to care about what his visits do to me.

"What? Who thinks that?"

"Everyone. Everyone at school. And I've been wondering, too." I bite my lip, deciding if I should go on.

"I've told you what happened," he says sharply. "You know what I was dealing with. There's no way I could have stopped it."

I've been wondering if that's true, but I can't tell him that—not yet. "Well, they think you killed yourself and they talk about why you did it. And not just your friends. Everyone."

I let my words sink in. I let him mull over the thought of the entire school ignoring his football record in favor of gossip.

"You wouldn't believe the theories that went around. Some were really laughable. 'Michael was bipolar.' 'Michael only had one month to live.' But don't feel too bad, it was purely defensive. People needed to find the flaws they'd missed when you were alive, because if the great Michael Green couldn't handle things, how is everybody else supposed to?"

"Well, at least you know the truth," he says.

I've wounded him and catch myself before a satisfied smile emerges on my face. I'm long past trying to understand what Michael does to me. Making me wish he were here in my room—in my bed—again, then the next minute making me relish the hurt in his voice. But I won't beat myself up for bruising his ego. He's made me his prisoner every night, and I'm glad when I can get a dig in.

"Damn it!" he growls, startling me. "I'm sick of talking. Let me in!"

He suddenly shifts his weight and slaps his palms against the glass. I flinch like it's me he's hit. I try to shrink away from him and sink into the mattress. God, why did I say those things?

My mouth dries to paper as I suck in the cold air pouring in over the sill. I make myself as small as possible and freeze into place. So far the window has barred his way. But that damn inch. I imagine him with new cat eyes that can see in the dark, noticing the currents of air playing around the opening. Does he know what I did—can he see? Is that small opening invitation enough for him to enter?

"Jordan," he croons. "I'm sorry. I'm so sorry. I didn't mean to scare you. I just miss you so much. I just want to be with you."

He jumps down to the ground, and I melt into the bed.

I'm shaking, but I won't pull up the blanket. I need to feel the cold; I need to feel something besides the ache I get when he leaves me. I hate myself for wanting him, for feeling flattered it's me he haunts every night.

Three months now I've talked to him through the window. Three months I've conjured his face from the time when he was mine. I see his chestnut eyes, his brown curls, his white, white teeth, and full mouth. I put that face on over the shadows and imagine we could start over.

But the leaves are falling and soon Michael will sit on bare branches. Moonlight will finally find its way to his face, and I'll see what I know is true: that Michael is a monster.

I'm just afraid that one of these nights I might let him in.

ABOUT THE AUTHOR

AMANDA MARRONE grew up on Long Island, where she spent her time reading, drawing, watching insects, and suffering from an overactive imagination. She earned a BA in education at SUNY Cortland and taught fifth and sixth grades in New Hampshire. She now lives in Connecticut with her husband, Joe, and their two kids. You can read more about Amanda Marrone's work at www.amandamarrone.com.

Check your PULSE

Simon & Schuster's **Check Your Pulse**
e-newsletter delivers current updates on
the hottest titles, exciting sweepstakes, and
exclusive content from your favorite authors.

Visit **TEEN.SimonandSchuster.com** to
sign up, post your thoughts, and find out what
every avid reader is talking about!

ATHENEUM

Margaret K. McElderry Books

Simon & Schuster
Books for Young Readers

SIMON
PULSE